THEY ARE AMER...
HOPE ...
SHA...

T... ...AUDERS

CAPTAIN "CRAZY JACK" KEENAN—The ultimate warrior, he doesn't need a weapon. He *is* a weapon.

SERGEANT CHAN—A deadly marksman who never misses.

LIEUTENANT THOMAS BEE—A Native American and Vietnam veteran, he has two favorite weapons, the mini crossbow and the Ninja shuriken.

CPO FREDDIE MAMUDI—A knife-wielding Afghani freedom fighter.

LIEUTENANT KINSKI—A human death machine who rocks-and-rolls with an assault rifle instead of a guitar.

Trained by the Guardians, America's elite commandos, they thought they had seen it all. But nothing could have prepared them for the Apocalyptic hell of a devastated Europe. Now, the ultimate battle begins . . .

THE MARAUDERS series
from Jove

THE MARAUDERS

Watch for

BLOOD KIN

coming in December!

MICHAEL McGANN

THE MARAUDERS

JOVE BOOKS, NEW YORK

THE MARAUDERS

A Jove Book/published by arrangement with
the author

PRINTING HISTORY
Jove edition / October 1989

ISBN: 0-515-10150-8

Jove Books are published by The Berkley Publishing Group,
200 Madison Avenue, New York, New York 10016.
The name "JOVE" and the "J" logo
are trademarks belonging to Jove Publications, Inc.

PRINTED IN THE UNITED STATES OF AMERICA

10 9 8 7 6 5 4 3 2 1

For the Los Angeles V.V.S.
and the good work they do

ONE

Willis MacGregor huddled at the fog-shrouded duck pond in the center of Hyde Park. In the distance Big Ben chimed twelve midnight. MacGregor didn't like London very much. He was a Scot. And, to a true Scot, every monument in England represented another chapter of servitude for the Scottish people.

He hadn't liked London before World War III, and he sure as hell didn't like it any more *now*.

He shivered as the damp crawled up his trouser legs and insinuated itself in his belly. Anxious, he ran his good left hand through his mane of curly red hair. He then fingered the battered remains of his right hand, now no more than twisted flesh housed in a studded leather glove. He found himself smirking. How did he, a cop and a son of a cop, wind up being a post-nuke Freedom Fighter?

Blind rage, really. Nothing more. Nothing more grandiose or noble. He was tired of being fucked about by forces that were totally beyond his control.

He rubbed the studded glove.

A gift from the powers that be.

He marveled over how his life had been altered by people he had barely heard of, let alone known.

A few years back some buffoon of a United States president,

with inflation and rampant unemployment nipping at his heels, decided to bolster his flagging popularity with inflammatory rhetoric aimed at the Soviet Union. The hell with the national deficit. Screw the international trade imbalance. Give the people what they want—saber-rattling. In a sense, his plan worked. He was perceived as a hero. The bastard even got reelected.

Nobody in the world took the President's verbal diarrhea seriously. Nobody except the Russians.

Glasnost iced over, and the Cold War was on again—in a very *hot* way.

The end of the world started with a milk run. Everybody ran them. Every Monday or every Friday—depending on what design your flag was—planes went up and played chicken with the opposition's radar. You found out what they had, and they figured out that you were still in the Game. No big deal. Two bunches of guys checking out the size of their military peckers.

One fateful day, however, one plane, a U.S. spotter, went in a little too close and shots were fired. First the spotter went down; then the Russians got burned by the spotter's high cover.

Maybe a dozen air jockeys on both sides went down in flames.

The Russians retaliated . . . in a big way. What had been a military exercise in East Germany became a hot, hard probe of NATO defenses. The U.S. rattled its Pershings, and the Soviets went all the way. They pushed the big red button.

Imagine the world's chagrin.

The Russians didn't care.

They simultaneously targeted 1,054 U.S. ICBM silos, 54 SAC bases and 2 SSBN bases. Their strategy was simple. By wiping out all the key military installations in the U.S., they would bring America to its knees without totally destroying the country. A weak America would be a useful America. Only America didn't play along.

The President, in a spirit of Sly Stallone-ism, played his part like a true ex-CIA hero. He launched everything America had. Contrary to some stories, the mushrooms were not red, white and blue. They were just bright. White hot. Devastating. Red. Bloody red. The blood of the innocent, of course.

The move tossed the concept of a limited nuclear war out the window.

When the Soviets saw that their strike would hit nothing but empty silos and deserted airfields, they launched a second salvo aimed at the most populous cities in the U.S.A.

They had nothing to lose anymore.

Another Soviet salvo took out most of Europe's key military bases.

And, for good measure, they launched "malice missiles," aimed at some of the oldest, most cultured cities in free Europe.

It was bigger and better than any Fourth of July celebration.

A lovely combination of nuclear and conventional strikes.

World War III was a draw. There were no winners. Only losers. Russia was obliterated, all of its cities gone; its prime land was poisoned for generations to come. The United States was half-destroyed, with various pieces held together by the acting President of the United States, MacGregor's distant cousin, Jeffrey. He ruled the land from an underground complex known as *Heartland*, located in north-central Iowa. The country was struggling to survive as best it could.

Western Europe had been spared, largely, from most of the big nuke blasts. What it hadn't been spared, however, was tyranny. Tyranny so subtle that some actually perceived it as normalcy. The tyranny was the brainchild of General Yevgeny Maximov, the only important survivor of the Soviet regime. A schemer. A dashing manipulator. A former member of the KGB.

Rallying the remnants of the Red Army, he marched across Eastern Europe and into the west, systematically destroying the governments of the surviving countries and installing hand-picked successors, successors who would pledge allegiance to the newly formed Federated States of Europe.

Many of the shell-shocked residents of Western Europe found the large, bearded Maximov the perfect solution to the post-nuclear chaos. He was charismatic. He was strong. He was friendly. MacGregor shivered in the damp; Maximov was friendly like Hitler had been friendly.

Still, for many people, the Federated government was a welcome relief from food shortages, sickness, the feeling of helplessness that permeated their lives in the first months following the war.

MacGregor tried hard for four years to let his feelings about international concerns slide. He lived in a small village outside Edinburgh. He learned to cope. To raise crops for survival. To deal with the fifteen-month-long nuclear winter. To handle the fact that most of the livestock would be poisoned for a generation or more.

But now Scotland was in danger.

And, in a way, so was America.

Still a cop, he had to march side by side with the Federated "invaders," Maximov's men, now clad in every military and police uniform that existed in Europe.

He rubbed a hand over his gnarled stump. The new king, one of Maximov's flunkies, was very good at exacting loyalty from his men.

Before the "coronation," MacGregor had a strong right fist. When the police force and the military had been reorganized, it was necessary to make examples of men who didn't respect the king enough.

They took away his hand and his rank.

Still, they allowed him to remain on the force. After all, he was a local. And a loyal local would keep his neighbors in line. So MacGregor was still a cop.

And, as a cop, MacGregor heard things.

Information privy only to the Federated boys. Information easily obtained after slipping one or two of the Czech sergeants one dram too many of the fine Scottish whiskey.

The information was slow in coming at first, MacGregor wheedled it out of his "companions," just for the hell of it. Just to pass the time. But when he found out too much, when he found out how strong the Federated States was growing, he felt his insides turn. For two weeks he felt like he would vomit his guts out during every waking hour.

What he knew was crucial. Lethal.

Using his police contacts, he sent a message off to his cousin in America. Then, through a network of old-time police informants, he managed to make contact with a small group of dissidents in the south.

His back to the wall, he was forced to take action. Forced to become militant. That's what brought him to London at midnight. And that's what made him so uneasy.

He was an outsider in London, yet he had not heard so much as a peep from the Eastern-Europeanized Scotland Yard. He was being set up and he knew it.

In London he was supposed to meet a contact, Clancy, who would pass him all the legal documents that would get him into Heathrow. After that, he was supposed to meet a Brit underground member named Ramsey. He had the address. It was on Baker Street, not far from the legendary address of Sherlock Holmes, now a business office.

Ramsey would give him the latest information on the FSE's plans and a timetable.

After that, MacGregor was on his own. He could board the private jet headed across the Atlantic and take his chances, or he could turn tail and run back to lush, green Scotland.

MacGregor heard a rustling in the bushes. A few of the swans in the park bleated nervously. He flattened himself behind a tree and watched a very well-dressed young man emerge from the bushes. He allowed the man to walk freely for a few yards before wrapping a mighty arm around his neck.

"I haven't got any money! I swear to God! You can have my food ration coupons. They're yours. They're yours!" the young man whined.

MacGregor released his grip.

He stared at the gagging little wimp. "Are you Clancy?" he muttered.

The shaking whelp stared up into the face of the red-haired titan. "Yes. Yes. Are you the one they call Shatterhand?"

MacGregor nodded. "You have the papers?"

Clancy nodded. He shoved an envelope of documents at MacGregor. MacGregor studied them. They seemed "official" enough. "Thanks."

He turned to walk away. Clancy tugged at his sleeve. "Wait a minute!"

MacGregor looked down at the skittish man. Clancy chuckled nervously. "Well, I mean, you can't just leave here . . . on your own."

"I'm not alone," MacGregor said flatly.

"But, your plans. You must have plans."

"That I have."

"Well, as one member of the Underground to another, you can tell me, right? I mean, we're both out to smash Yevgeny."

"Yevgeny?"

"Chairman Maximov."

"I don't care one way or the other about the *Chairman*, son," MacGregor said. "I've never met him."

"But what he *stands* for, I mean," Clancy injected, a little too quickly.

MacGregor nodded. He knew, now, why no one had stopped him from walking the street after curfew. Why no police had patrolled the Park.

"Yes, I will tell you my plans," he said. "But not here. Not out in the open."

Clancy attempted a smile. "Well, where then? We can't leave the park."

"The bandshell," MacGregor said.

"Fine. Let's go."

The two men walked along the pond toward the pristine white bandshell; a small edifice where, a nuclear lifetime ago, local and national bands had played long and loud for both the people and the Royal Family.

When there had been a Royal Family.

They had been "disappeared" shortly after the creation of the Federated States of Europe; replaced by acne-scarred King Edward.

The two men walked to the bandshell.

"Now, what have you got for me?" Clancy asked.

"This," MacGregor said, lifting his studded right stump. He brought it down heavily on the young man's head. He heard the skull crunch, felt the exhale of air. Clancy crumpled onto the ground, moaning softly.

MacGregor saw the man's legs tremble. The wiry body began to convulse. He hesitated. No, this was no time for mercy. He raised his studded stump and brought it down again and again and again on the traitor's head.

After a few moments there was very little of the man's head left.

MacGregor walked, casually, to the pond and washed the

bits of semi-solid matter from his leather-encased stump. He then padded through the bushes. Where there was bait, there was backup, he reasoned.

Reaching into his long raincoat, he produced a Walther MPK Model S. He swung the folding stock around until it clicked into place. Very carefully he walked through the park.

He heard the squawk of a radio.

Crouching, he saw two dozen of Britain's new police, mostly Eastern Europeans, wearing traditional British bobby outfits but carrying AK-47s, a gift from the remnants of the Russian army. A badly scarred sergeant chattered into a walkie-talkie. "He's made contact," he said in a heavily accented voice, "but there's still no word."

The walkie-talkie belched back.

"Fine. Yes, sir. If we don't hear from him in five minutes, we go in."

MacGregor sighed.

Clearly, for the police, this was to be a routine execution. MacGregor was not a big threat, simply an annoying gnat, something very squashable. The police weren't highly alert. After all, they were after one lone traitor, a cripple at that.

He was about 1,000 feet from the men. He knew that the weapon was good for 1,600 feet. He slipped in the magazine and settled the gunstock against his cheek. Rising slowly, he opened fire, catching the men by surprise. He sprayed the area, 550 rounds per minute.

The "police" leaped up, going for their weapons, when the first fusillade of screaming lead sliced through the delicate shrubbery of Hyde Park.

The branches of the bushes broke and splintered.

For the men, it wasn't as simple.

Their bodies spun violently as MacGregor advanced, still firing. The air around him sizzled with the crack-crack-cracking of the gun.

The police twisted and turned before him, like marionettes with their strings entangled. All the police hit the ground, still shaking, still spewing blood.

MacGregor kept firing.

Small cyclones of dirt and grit churned up from the ground. MacGregor continued to advance, tears dribbling down his cheeks. He thought of the world as it once had been. He

thought of families in the Northland, happy, back then, to
eek out a living on their farms. He thought of them, now.
Facing poisoned ground. Dying livestock. Feeling the first
effects of the Lingering Sickness. He thought of their babies,
born twisted limbed and weak and dying within weeks.

He thought of a smiling Maximov, living somewhere in the
east, in a luxurious castle.

He thought of Scotland's own castles, now used as emergency hospitals to house the mounting number of terminally
ill.

The soldiers lay sprawled on the ground before him, dead
and dying. MacGregor stood above them, his rage ever increasing. He fired into their lifeless bodies, chewing up their
features in spray after spray of bullets. When he was done,
he stuck in another cartridge and fired again.

Ammunition spent, he slowly lowered his gun and gazed
down at the carnage. He didn't feel heroic. He didn't feel
guilt. He didn't feel anything. In the back of his mind he
heard the sirens. More police were en route.

Tucking the gun down at his side, he strode out of Hyde
Park, the whirling, swirling fog clinging to his ankles.

He had to find a man named Ramsey.

He had to flee his homeland, the place where his heart
would always be.

He had to journey to Heartland.

Like his ancestors before him, he would leave his past
behind and strike out across the Atlantic.

Willis MacGregor was going to America.

And when he returned to Europe, he'd make Maximov and
his stooges wish they had never been born.

TWO

They were called The Guardians . . . and the fate of America was in their hands.

In the four years since World War III had exploded across the earth, an elite team of men hand-picked by former Vice President, now President, Jeffrey MacGregor, had fought a continuous series of guerrilla battles to keep the country intact.

The four men—Wilson, McKay, Rogers and Sloan—had largely kept the remnants of the United States together, beating down any and all insurrectionist groups that arose from within and without the country, while President MacGregor went about the task of pulling the country up, once again, under provisions made in a secret Blueprint for Renewal.

It had been a month since the President had received an urgent communiqué from a distant cousin across the Atlantic.

It had been a week since his cousin had arrived.

During this short time the President had to totally reevaluate his plans for the future. It wasn't good enough to merely rebuild America. America had to be made safe from its foes across the sea. Something had to be done and done quickly if what Willis MacGregor said was true.

A second elite squad had to be formed and formed quickly; an elite squad that would operate in the Euro-theater, an elite

9

squad that, thousands of miles from Heartland, would virtually be on its own for months at a time, maybe years. An elite squad that faced the impossible task of sabotaging the inner workings of the Federated States of Europe. An elite squad that very well could meet instant failure and a slow death.

The President had asked Commander Sam Sloan of the Guardians to locate five of the toughest fighters the armed forces had ever known.

Sloan, a young man with a deceptively shy smile, was a Navy ace and probably the most levelheaded of the Guardians. Where other men blew up with rage, Sloan merely simmered. What he physically lacked in bulk, he made up for in terms of sheer, iron determination.

The President sat in his office in Heartland; his intercom buzzed. He bent over to answer the squawk box and caught a glimpse of himself in his polished desktop. He cringed. Four years ago, he had been the fair-haired, handsome boy, the young liberal to balance a presidential ticket. These days, he looked more like Rose Kennedy than JFK. His face was deeply lined, his eyes nearly always puffy. He wore his fatigue like a suit of armor.

"Yes?" he said into the intercom.

"Commander Sloan is here, Mr. President," the box belched. "He has some . . . men . . . with him."

"Fine," the President said. "Take them to the conference room. We'll meet there in five minutes. And send for my cousin. Ask him to join us in a half hour."

The President eased back into his chair and shut his eyes for a moment, recalling what the presidency had once meant to him. The leader of a mighty nation. Gazing out of the White House onto the sprawl known as Washington, D.C. The Lincoln Monument. The Capitol Building. The Vietnam Memorial.

Now, somewhere out there, in the aboveworld, they lay in ruins.

He got to his feet and walked toward the door. Government sure wasn't what it used to be.

THREE

When the President arrived, Commander Sam Sloan was already present, his lanky form twisted up into the equivalent of a question mark. He flashed the President, a lopsided grin, and in a Missouri twang that betrayed both pride and a great sense of anxiety, he announced, "Mr. President, these are the men you requested."

The President nodded at the five men in the room. He knew, now, why Sloan appeared so nervous. The five men in the room resembled a rogues' gallery more than a group of elite fighters.

"You may be seated, gentlemen." The President smiled.

The five men slid into chairs around the conference room's massive, oblong table. If they were impressed with meeting the President, they didn't show it. Sloan dropped a sheaf of folders in front of the President.

"Gentlemen, you've all been briefed as to why you've been requested. I thank you for coming on such short notice. I'll review your records, then you'll be further briefed. At the end of the briefing, any man who wishes not to take part in this action will be free to go."

The men grunted by way of response.

The President felt a migraine coming on. A bad one. He

opened the first folder. "Captain John F. Keenan," he intoned.

"Crazy Jack," a mountain of a man with flaming red hair corrected. "My buddies call me Crazy Jack, sir."

The President looked up. Crazy Jack Keenan stood six feet four inches tall and weighed 230 pounds. He had a 32-inch waist, and in another time, would have fit in perfectly at California's Muscle Beach. He resembled a well-tailored brick. Ruddy complexion. Ice blue eyes. The President smiled at Keenan. This man didn't need a weapon. He *was* a weapon.

"Fine, Crazy Jack," the President said. "Do you mind if I read aloud from your record?"

"Nope . . . *sir*," Crazy Jack grinned.

The President chuckled. "Former Green Beret captain. West Point grad. Three tours in Nicaragua."

"I wanted four," Crazy Jack winked, " 'cause I loved the climate. But my *superiors* thought it wouldn't be good for my mental hygiene."

"So I see," the President nodded. "You've been in the brig more times than most of Reagan's cabinet members."

"I was prone to discussions in bars." Keenan grinned sheepishly.

"Uh-huh," the President nodded. "Seems as though you had a weakness for going AWOL, too."

"Only on weekends."

"Came close to a Bad Conduct Discharge three times."

"Small beer."

"Evidently," the President said. "The only thing that saved you was your record. Impressive military record . . . Crazy Jack. Plus, you're a smart fellow. A combined M.S. in chemistry and physics. Mother's named Christina Agnes McCarthy. Father's name, Josef Kennaczewski."

"Yeah, he had it shortened when he came to America in the thirties," Jack said.

"Why? He was Ukrainian. Surely he . . ."

"He was an asshole." Jack shrugged. "And he couldn't spell."

"Well, Jack" the President said. "Judging by your record, I'm delighted you're here."

Jack glanced at his companions. "Had nothing much else

to do. I mean, since the war and all I've had a lot of time on my hands. Not too many people want a mercenary who's also good in physics.''

The President opened the second file. ''Lieutenant Thomas Bee.''

A tan, six-foot slab of a man with shouder-length black hair nodded. He said nothing. He merely glared at the President.

''You're an Indian,'' the President said.

''Native American,'' Bee said in a monotone. ''Hopi.''

''Taos is your hometown?''

Bee nodded. Tom Bee had the strength of a tree and his limbs were just as sinewy. He projected the aura of the Eternal Outsider. That was a trait the President could identify with. ''A Vietnam veteran. Congressional Medal of Honor. Two Purple Hearts. First Marine Division. Participated in Operation SHELBY.''

''September twenty-first to twenty-eighth, Cau Lau Trung on Goi Noi Island.''

''Your methods were pretty unorthodox, Thomas. Illegal weaponry. Mini cross-bow. Ninja shuriken.''

''Old habits,'' Tom Bee said flatly.

''You seem to have excellent qualifications as a fighting man.''

''And a teacher,'' Bee muttered.

''What?''

''I teach children. At the village. I taught children. How to live in peace with the Earth. With the Sun. Sister Moon. Brother Sea.''

''I see,'' the President muttered.

Tom offered a smirk, as if to say ''I doubt it.'' ''It's really hard to teach that path these days. The Earth is poison. The sun is too hot. The moon is often blotted out with clouds of soot and debris, and the sea is rising, its life dying. I suppose you could say I was a teacher of fantasy.''

''Well, thank you for coming, Thomas.''

''You're welcome,'' Bee said evenly.

''Gunnery Sergeant Winston S. Chan, United States Marine Corps.''

A short, muscular, but decidedly rotund bald man saluted. ''Glad to be here, *sir*,'' he said from behind a pair of gold shooter's glasses. "And, if I may be permitted, sir, *my* friends call me Buddha Chan."

"All right, Buddha Chan," the President said. "Let's see. Your family was living in Ulan Bator, Outer Mongolia."

"We were driven from there by the Soviets, *sir*," Chan said. "My father was a local Ford dealer. He was considered a capitalist. They shot him. My mother and I moved to the States."

"Yes, I see," the President said. "And even after the war, you remained in the Corps."

"This is my country, sir. My mother died in the last war. She would have wanted me to protect and to serve my President."

"You have an incredible record of marksmanship, Buddha."

"The best sniper in the Corps, *sir*," Chan smiled thinly, turning his beach-ball face into a "have a nice day" poster. "My record backs my statement."

"Indeed, it does," the President said, moving on to another file.

"Chief Petty Officer Farouz Mamudi."

"Freddie, sir."

"Fine, Freddie," the President glanced up. Slender and attractive, except for a long scar that ran from his hairline down over his glass eye, Mamudi was a devout Sunni Muslim, one of the kind who respected the religion of others, but who burned to free his homeland from the Federated States.

"You're a former Navy SEAL from the Kazahk SSR adajacent to Afghanistan."

"Yes, Mr. President," the wiry, one-eyed man replied, his head bobbing in birdlike movements.

"You have an infirmity."

"Glass eye, Mr. President," Freddie grinned, popping out his brown orb and plopping in an eye bearing a little green frog with a sailor hat, a SEAL symbol.

"I have a lot of replacements, guaranteed to break the ice at parties."

The man motioned to his eye and the scar. "Became a pop-eye the same time I got my zipper. Soviet sniper. He fired. I ducked. I was slower. What a world, huh?"

"Your record seems impeccable . . . except for . . ."

"They never proved the morals charge, Mr. President," Freddie beamed. "In my religion, multiple wives are allowed. I tried to acquire at least one or two wherever I was stationed."

"Well, Freddie," the President sighed, "would that hinder your assignment in Europe?"

"Not unless there are no more women there," Freddie said, resting his thin chin on an extended palm.

"Lieutenant Peter Kinski," the President intoned. "USAF."

"Present, sir," a tall, lanky blond man with a hairful of mousse nodded. Kinski wore his hair like a 1950s rock idol. Rumor had it that in battle he worried more about losing his comb than his life.

"It says here that you were called 'Silver Tongue' by your peers."

"Yes, sir."

"Why is that?"

"I lie a lot, sir."

The President massaged his eyelids. His headache was getting worse. "Polish descent. Electronics expert. Fine flyer. Anything I've left out?"

"I have a weakness for one thing Russian, sir."

"What's that?"

"An AK-47 folding stock assault rifle. It can cut anything in two, and it's better than the shit we used in the service."

"Thank you, Kinski."

"You're welcome, sir."

The President closed the last of the files. He faced the five men: Crazy Jack, Tom Bee, Winston Chan, Freddie Mamudi and Kinski. "As of today, gentleman, if you so choose, you will be a unit. A pilot team for a larger Special Forces detachment that will come in and continue to bolster the pockets of resistance that you find, locate and lead in Europe."

"Excuse me, sir," Crazy Jack said, raising a massive hand like an overgrown schoolboy. "But don't we have enough problems here at home? I mean . . . why worry about Europe?"

The President pressed an intercom button before him on the table. "We *do* have enough problems over here, Crazy Jack. But we have even more problems in Europe."

He faced the intercom. "Send in my cousin."

The door to the room opened, and Willis MacGregor, six feet six, forty-five years old, red hair glistening and wearing a traditional Scottish kilt, entered the room.

"He'll tell you about it," the President said.

Crazy Jack chuckled at the fellow whose hair was almost as red as his. "Hey, Mac, didn't anyone tell you the miniskirt look is out?"

MacGregor said not a word. He walked up to the table where Crazy Jack sat and, raising his steel-studded stump, sent it smashing down onto and into the mahogany top.

He glared down at massive Crazy Jack. "I didn't come here to fuck around, Yank."

Crazy Jack gulped and, turning to a stone-faced Tom Bee, nodded. "I like this guy. I really do."

"I'm so glad, lad," the older, more cantankerous Scot said, yanking his stump out of the table.

"My *cousin*," the President said, "will tell you why he made the long journey to Heartland."

MacGregor walked to a spot directly behind where the President was sitting. He folded his massive arms. "Friends," he said, "I'm not a soldier or a sailor or a flying boy. I am Willis MacGregor and I'm just a normal man. A policeman. My family has lived in a small village in Scotland for the last three hundred years. This is my first . . . *vacation* abroad."

"Didn't pick such a great time to come," Crazy Jack muttered.

"Shhh," stout Chan hissed.

"I came because I *had* to. Right now, this country, *your* country, is on the brink of destruction."

"How is that?" Freddie Mamudi asked.

"As you probably all know," MacGregor said, bouncing up and down on the balls of his feet, "Europe has been taken over by the Federated States."

"Chairman Maximov," the Guardian's Sloan muttered.

"Exactly," MacGregor said. "A man I think you're aware of."

Sloan nodded. The other men in the room grew grave. MacGregor continued. "Maximov has moved into every country in Europe, flattering, cajoling, executing. He has installed puppet governments everywhere. There are feudal systems, regal systems, 'democratic' systems . . . but they all are controlled by Maximov. Right now, there are three key henchmen in Western Europe: Giles Robespierre, Sven Lundgren and, in my area, a twit by the name of Ian O'Malley. He's headquartered in Ireland.

"Technically, the United Kingdom is controlled by a sop named Edward. King Edward. But it's O'Malley that's calling the shots."

"This is very interesting," Tom Bee said passively, "but why are you here? Why do you need us?"

MacGregor stared at the soft-spoken Hopi. "Mr. O'Malley is assembling a massive buildup of troops and supplies in the South of England. Their aim? To march through the northland, through *my* homeland, Scotland, and re-start the massive oil platforms in the North Sea."

"So?" Crazy Jack shrugged. "We all know that the FSE's been bent on production."

"Right you are, boy," MacGregor spat back. "But this time, the reason is a tad more sinister than normal. O'Malley, *Maximov*, want to gear up, for the first time since the last war, a series of refineries that will produce the basis of jet fuel. Fuel for a recently discovered cache of British air force planes lying dormant in Ireland.

"Put it together, boy. One aircraft carrier, which they have, and a squadron of planes, which they have . . . and *you* don't . . . and what does that equal?"

"Invasion," Mamudi whispered.

"Exactly." MacGregor nodded. "At least the beginnings of a logical one. And the more ships and the more planes they salvage, the bigger the invasion will be. There are plans afloat to resurface the American nuclear fleet that was sunk in Scotland. I don't think you have the capabilities, right about now, to stop them.

"Our beloved King Edward is attempting to rally the support of the people. He's laying on a lot of rhetoric about how Post-Nuke America has turned against its allies. He's reaching home in the younger ones, the skinheads. There's a large anti-American, pro-FSE base growing in the U.K. They're young. They're angry. They don't know any better.

"Some of the older folks, people like me, people my parents' age, who remember World War II and still see the

Americans as their allies are trying to hold the fort . . . but it's a losing battle. America, you see, has been conspicuous by its absence since the last big war.''

"We were nuked!" Crazy Jack declared.

"A lot of people over there aren't aware of that," MacGregor said. "They don't know the extent of the damage. In the eyes of Europe, *you* are responsible for the last war.''

"Great," Mamudi muttered.

"And I bet," Kinski offered, "that it's the same old story over there. The kids don't have jobs. They have nowhere to go. So they join the army or the navy. They're getting paid. They don't care who the enemy is as long as there's an enemy.''

MacGregor smiled. "Smart lad. So America is the target. What do we do?''

"We don't have the firepower to go in there and take them out," Kinski said.

"No," MacGregor replied. "But if a group of the finest fighting men, the greatest guerrillas your government can muster, goes in to rally what *true* patriots are left . . . we have a shot. And in Scotland, you have a fine shot to stop the oil refineries. The clans.''

"The guys in white sheets?" Crazy Jack marveled.

"No," MacGregor laughed, "the guys in mini-skirts.''

All the men at the table laughed. MacGregor raised his good fist proudly. He scanned the room. "Clans, my boys. Families. Groups that have been together for hundreds of years, defending their country from the British. They've gone underground since the war. Retreated. Nursing their villages, their families, through the aftermath. But if we can get them together, encourage them to fight back the FSE gangs, not just for Scotland, but for the *world*, then we can nip our nouveau-Reds in the bloody bud.''

"I like this guy," Crazy Jack cackled. "I really do.''

"And, Mr. Crazy Jack''—MacGregor beamed—"please don't feel compelled to play the macho Morlock with me. I'm pretty well read, for a cop. In case you didn't know, we have one of the finest educational systems in Europe. I know a lot about you. Your books on New Age Physics were pretty interesting.''

Crazy Jack blushed. "I didn't think anyone read them.''

"*I* did."

Crazy Jack grew redder. "And you liked them?"

"Very much. So just in case we wind up working together, don't play the part of the mindless tough guy. Tough, you may be. Mindless, you aren't."

"You're all right, Mac." Crazy Jack smiled.

"I get by," MacGregor replied.

"What are we up against?" Bee asked.

"Everything and more. The FSE boys have all the guns and all the ammo they 'appropriated' from the armed forces of the countries they took over. In addition, they raided just about every commerial weaponry facility. There's a bit of mix and match in their forces, but they get along quite nicely. And, what they lack in guns, they make up for in . . . let's say . . . spirit."

He removed the studded leather glove from his fist. He held up what was left of his right hand. It was gray and scarred, looking more like a rotting vegetable than any human appendage.

"This was a little memento I received from my king for not taking him very seriously very quickly."

The men around the room shivered involuntarily.

"It's amazing what a little battery acid will do." MacGregor nodded, replacing his glove. "And I'm a *nobody*. I'm not a hero like you all are."

"A hero is a sandwich," Crazy Jack said, feeling an instant kinship with the burly Scot.

MacGregor grinned, holding up his hand. "This is nothing," he said. "All it lost me was a hand, gained me a nickname as well. All the cops around the Edinburgh district call me 'Shatterhand.' But what the FSE is doing to the stalwarts, to the ones *really* opposed to their policies . . . well, the likes of it hasn't been seen since the Spanish Inquisition. Their methods are primitive, brutal and extremely effective. We're up against a very formidable enemy, my friends."

"They've got the guns," Kinski said.

"And the numbers," Chan added.

"So," Mamudi asked, "what have we got?"

"Hopefully," MacGregor said, "guts. Spirit. And, most importantly, *heart*."

MacGregor sat down next to his cousin, the President. The men in the room remained silent.

"Not much on tactics," Buddha said, rubbing his shaved head thoughtfully.

The President faced them all. "The odds aren't good, gentlemen. The danger will be to the maximum, the backup to the minimum. It's your choice."

"I'm in," Crazy Jack said, pounding a fist on the table. "I'd love to go to the Ukraine some day and kick Maximov's men out on their ass."

"I'll fight," Kinski said. "Screw it. I'm a Polack. I don't know any better."

Mamudi laughed. "I don't care about odds. You all know the story of the Crusades? Once, Richard the Lionhearted met with the great Suleiman the Magnificent for a parlay. Richard brought along his strongest warrior. The warrior split a two-foot-long wooden block with an English broadsword. 'Can you do that with your blades?' Richard asked, glancing at the thin sword sheathed by Suleiman.

" 'No,' Suleiman said. He whipped off his silk scarf and allowed it to drift across the blade of his upturned scimitar. The scimitar cleanly severed the cloth as it fell to the ground. 'Can you do that with yours?' I am in this. Sometimes the smallest weapon is the most effective."

Chan chuckled at that. "Buddha Chan has never backed off from anybody at any time. I am in, with pleasure, *sir*."

All eyes were on Tom Bee. The Hopi stared straight ahead. "We have taken the earth and we have ruined it. Raped it. Now is the time to rebuild. And to rebuild, we need growers, not enslavers. I, Thomas Bee, will be proud to serve with you, Mr. MacGregor . . . , and kick some ass."

MacGregor and the President heaved a sigh. Sam Sloan gazed on the men proudly. "I wish I could go with you guys, I really do."

Crazy Jack cackled. "You'll have your hands full at home, Commander. Just keep the homefires burning, because when we come marching back here, we're going to have one blowout of a party."

"Amen," Chan seconded.

Sloan offered the men one last out. "Now, before you all go running off, you have to know the facts. Once you're in the boonies, you'll be out there on your own, with whatever the Scots can salvage. There won't be any amtracks to get you across marshes and swamps. You'll have to slog it like any grunt.

"APCs? No way. You'll be using whatever vehicles you can jury-rig. Air support? At this point, zilch. No Cobras, no B-52s, no Dragon Ships of any kind to get the FSE boys off your ass.

"You're starting from scratch, guys. I wish I could say otherwise."

The gathered men glanced at each other and offered a collective shrug. "So, what else is new?" Crazy Jack grinned.

The President gathered up the files. "Thank you, gentlemen. You will be leaving the day after tomorrow. As of now, you will be the first Special Forces team to infiltrate FSE territory. As of now, your code name will be *The Marauders*. Good luck and may God be with you."

Crazy Jack grinned as he slouched in his chair. "I have the feeling we're going to need both luck and fugging Jeezus to get us through this mess."

The other men at the table began to giggle like small children. By the time Sloan and the President left the room, the Marauders were roaring.

They weren't lost men, after all.

Somebody needed them, it seemed.

The people of the world.

FOUR

King Edward was nervous. His acne-besmirched face had flared up even more than usual since the slaughter in Hyde Park. He sat, pensive, in his room at Buckingham Palace. Sometimes he actually felt like a prisoner there.

In fact, he was.

However, when he compared his own life to the fate of the Royal Family preceding him, he figured that he didn't have it too bad. They had "disappeared" shortly after the FSE made inroads into England. Disappeared? Edward smirked. They had been captured in the middle of the night, their Special Air Service men and Royal Guards slaughtered. Throats slit, they had been dismembered and tossed into the Thames.

Fish food.

Not a trace left after two weeks.

How Chairman Maximov had picked Edward was beyond him. He had been a pimp and a drug runner, although his dear old grandmum claimed that she had been a descendant of the Tudor line. Actually, the family had been indentured servants back then, as far as Edward knew. Perhaps they had *worked* on one of the Tudor estates. More than likely, they had been tossed in jail for some offense or another and they gave the Tudor name as the name of their employer. No matter. The name had stuck.

22

He was king now.

That was a lot better than running women and crack.

It was probably his close association with O'Malley that turned the trick. O'Malley was the FSE's majordomo in the area, and formerly Edward Tudor's boss in the drug racket.

Edward stiffened when he heard the knock at the door. The door burst open, nearly sending Edward into a seizure.

Ian O'Malley and his most trusted lieutenant, Sean Carter, marched into the room.

"Sweet Jeezus," Edward exclaimed, "you nearly gave me a heart attack, Ian."

"Shut up, Eddie," O'Malley said, striding across the room like a hybrid of James Cagney and the leader of the Wee Folk. "You have a drink about?"

King Edward, his knees knocking, pointed to a small minibar in the corner. O'Malley poured himself three fingers of Scotch and downed it. Carter, his stooge, stood in the corner, a long, gaunt man.

O'Malley didn't offer him a drink.

"We're in big trouble, Eddie," O'Malley said. "The Hyde Park slaughter has put a major glitch in the operations."

"It was just one gunman," Edward replied. "There's no sign of any *movement*, anti-government, I mean."

"I know what you mean," O'Malley said, pouring himself another drink. "And if your head was any more up your ass, you'd be using your pecker as a periscope."

"Excuse me," Edward said, standing. "I am your *king*. Watch how you speak to me."

"You are a twit," O'Malley said. "And don't ever forget it. That's the only reason you're sitting on someone else's bloody throne."

Edward lowered himself back into the sofa. He gaped at the room. It was beyond ornate. Priceless paintings and relics dating back from the mid-1500s. He wouldn't like to lose all this. "Sorry, Ian," he muttered.

"We have to get ourselves a story together before the Chairman arrives," O'Malley muttered.

"Maximov?" Edward gulped. "Here?"

"Any hour. Any minute. Any fuggin' second."

"Jesus!" Edward gasped.

"Maximov's bad enough," Ian cracked. "We still have no idea about the identity of the shooter?"

"No," Edward said. "Scotland Yard is at a loss. From the way the bullets were fired . . ."

"The trajectory," Carter corrected.

"The, uh, tragic ectomy," Edward continued. "We know that he must have been a big one. He was firing down, ya see, so we . . ."

"I get the picture, Eddie," Ian said, wondering if this boy king was nothing more than the product of generation upon generation of first cousins breeding.

"Do we have any bodies, uh, political prisoners, we can fob this off on?" O'Malley asked.

"No," the king replied. "We've laid off the rough stuff for the last three months. Trying to better our image."

"*Your* image," O'Malley spat. "You're not old enough to use the royal 'we.' "

O'Malley danced his compact body into a stiff-backed chair. "Then, Eddie, old pal, we're up the creek without a paddle. We're dead meat."

"Do you think the Chairman will . . . ?" the king began.

"I *know* he will," O'Malley replied. "And more so."

A manservant, looking very much like a cartoon butler, staggered into the room, totally inebriated. "Yer Haghness, Chairmenz Maximoff awaits yer prezzenz downstairs. Missers O'Malley and Carter azz well."

"Tell them we'll be there in a moment," Edward said, rising and running to a mirror to straighten his straw-like hair.

"Hee sed *now*," the butler wheezed.

"Oh, very well. Tell them we'll be down . . . *now*."

The butler smirked at the Clearasil-clad king. "Twit," he muttered, turning on his heels and leaving.

"Now what?" the King asked.

"We have the fan. He has the shit," O'Malley shrugged. "We just have to see how far it flies and how fast we can duck."

FIVE

Such decadence, Yevgeny Maximov thought, sitting in the glittering parlor of Buckingham Palace, smoking his *makhorka* cigarette. He glanced at the furniture, the priceless tapestries, the world-renowned paintings.

He could have taken all of it back to his own castle, but he didn't have the room for it. Plus, he didn't really *respect* the British all that much. He had crushed them after the war without even using a closed fist. He had barely raised his political pinky, really.

He had been disappointed, in a way, that taking over the fragments of Europe had been so easy. All of Europe had been so *passive* about Maximov's rising to the Chairmanship of the Federated States. They were quite happy to entrust their fate to any fellow on horseback who rode through their lands.

Maximov had been the first one to gallop to their "rescue," promising law, order and normalcy.

It had not taken Maximov long to install his lackies in key positions—a very boring process, really, especially for a man like Maximov, who thrived on intrigue and game-playing. He rose from his chair and walked to the window.

London was such an *ugly* city. The worst of both worlds. Tacky, tasteless new skyscrapers and shopping complexes blended horribly, next to the skeletons of once-great buildings.

He took a puff on his cigarette. It tasted like horseshit. But Maximov, born a Ukrainian, refused to smoke any of the lesser, more American brands. You might as well have puffed on paper.

He straightened his massive form. Resembling a grizzly bear in a well-tailored suit, the bearded, balding Maximov furrowed his brow, thinking about how this idiot King of England had, inadvertently, set his plans for conquering America back months.

"Idiot," he whispered. "Syphilitic idiot."

"You called for me?" a voice chirped from the far side of the room.

Maximov turned and stared down at the anorexic form of trembling King Edward. Flanking him were the diminutive O'Malley and the skeletal Carter.

"Yes." Maximov grinned. "I did."

O'Malley was a good man, Maximov knew. Before the war, he had managed to be both a member of a British Intelligence Unit and the IRA; he had sold information to one, weapons to the other. He had managed to make a small fortune playing one side against the other. After the war, Maximov saw no reason to change O'Malley's lifestyle.

As Chief Lieutenant of the U.K. Sector, he offered bribes and bounties to the Northern Irish Catholics, Protestants and IRA extremists for capturing any weaponry they could donate to the FSE.

O'Malley had done a good job of keeping the United Kingdom dangling by the edge of its fingertips. Maximov had never feared an uprising in the area . . . until now.

Carter was a good man, too. A former SAS man, he had the instincts of a killer. What he lacked, however, was an overview of the politics of Europe at present.

He had allowed King Edward, a weiner who, as the monarch of the new U.K., had to be kept propped up, to let an insurrectionist go free. Not only that, he had allowed the insurrectionist to take out a big bunch of Britain's police force, actually East Germans.

"Please, gentlemen . . . Your Highness," Maximov smiled from behind his beard. "Be seated."

The three men, resembling the number 101, sat down on a single sofa.

"As you know," Maximov said, sucking on his dogshit cigarette, "the FSE is planning to begin a massive air force. The key to its survival is the reactivating of the oil platforms in the North Sea. It's going to take courage, resources and a sense of vision to make that journey. The terrain is rough. The local inhabitants are old-fashioned and not receptive to new ideas."

"Damn Scots," Edward muttered.

Maximov ignored him. "In spite of these difficulties, the FSE has vowed to journey north and locate and reopen these refineries. There are certain small pockets of resistance, but we know we can handle them. After all, our new king is the leader of his country, is he not?"

"Bloody right." Edward nodded.

Maximov grinned like a piranha. "Then, how is it, Your Highness, that one lone gunman, trying to make his way out of England to contact, I must assume, other dissidents, managed to wipe out twenty-one heavily armed policemen? Not to mention one valuable informant?"

King Edward shot O'Malley a nervous look.

O'Malley ignored him.

The King gulped. "I—I don't make much of that, Chairman Maximov. I mean, it was a lone crazy person. It was just dumb luck. It doesn't hamper the oil operation at all, duzzit? I mean, everything is still on schedule?"

"It may be." Maximov nodded. "But no thanks to the likes of you, Your Highness."

The king's eyes bulged. O'Malley sighed. He'd been in the slime-mold realm long enough to know what was coming next. He slid down in the sofa.

Maximov walked across the room, pulling a .357 magnum from inside his pocket. "And," he continued, "to show Your Highness how much this reconstituted air force, how much this potential first strike force, means to *me*, means to the FSE, I will demonstrate how, ummmm, *enthusiastic* I am about it all."

He turned to the skeletal Carter, a superb, loyal FSE supporter, raised his pistol and blew the man's skull off. Carter's body slid onto the lap of the thoroughly shocked king.

"Yccccch!" the king theorized, scrambling to his feet, allowing Carter's body to slide onto the floor with a numbed hiss of air.

The King stood there, shimmying. O'Malley sat there, disgusted.

Maximov towered before the two.

"I think I've proven how dedicated I am to successfully completing this mission. Now, I would advise you both: Find the man or the force planning to stop the North Sea Operation—or prepare to join Mr. Carter, there, on the floor. Good day, gentlemen."

Maximov lumbered toward the door, still puffing his cigarette. He turned one last time toward the two cowering men. "And, for the record, gentlemen, the weather around here *stinks*."

SIX

The Marauders sat uncomfortably in the reconverted DC-10. Once owned by a young, rich pop music manager (he had managed The Sex Slaves, Big Boobs, and The Large Faces featuring Rod LaMont, among others), the jet's interior had been trashed and painted bright pink. A bowling alley had been installed as well as a video arcade. Now it housed five expatriate heroes as well as a burly, crippled Scot.

"We'll be landing in Edinburgh instead of Heathrow," MacGregor said to the troops.

"Why the change in the LZ?" Gold Buddha asked.

"We've learned that London has gotten very *hot* since my dalliance in Hyde Park," MacGregor said.

"Great." Crazy Jack sighed. "We might as well be landing in a neon-lit display. I mean, this bucket isn't exactly the Stealth."

MacGregor ran his massive good hand through his curly red hair. "We had no choice." MacGregor sighed. "FSE troops have taken over the naval base at Rosyth in Fife . . ."

"Nuclear sub base, right?" Kinski injected.

"Right you are." MacGregor nodded. "They also have control of the NATO base on the Clyde and an RAF station at Kinloss. Any military vehicle that existed in Scotland is in the hands of the FSE. Fortunately, there's not enough fuel to go around, so in terms of air and sea power, they're pretty

29

poor. Still, with the FSE toadies roaming the area, it would've been damned difficult to hijack a military plane. We were lucky one of our London informants had connections with the remainder of the idle rich or we wouldn't have gotten our hands on this . . . 'bucket.' ''

Crazy Jack suddenly found his knees interesting. "No offense."

"None taken." MacGregor smiled. "It's not all as bad as that. There'll be a group of resistance men meeting us at the airport."

"We still have the element of surprise," Freddie said, adjusting a new glass eye, a skull and cross-bones ditty.

"How do you like the new peeper?" he asked Tom Bee.

The Hopi, the oldest of the crew, stared at the wiry young Muslim. "It's nice."

"Nice?" Freddie exclaimed. "It's magnificent. Do you know how much I *paid* to have this made?"

"Don't know," Tom Bee said, returning his attention to his weaponry. "Don't care."

"Just trying to be sociable," Freddie muttered.

Bee checked his survival/combat knife—a twelve-inch-long job with a serrated seven-inch blade and a black aluminum handle.

In his belt, he kept nine Ninja shuriken. A four-pointed star made of hardened steel, three and one half inches in diameter, it could be hurled at high speed by someone trained in martial arts. The points pierced the flesh. Aimed at vital organs, the shuriken could be very effective. Dipped in poison, its points could be lethal.

Bee also carried a mini-crossbow, approximately the size of a sawed-off shotgun. It came in very handy for stalking and fighting when he needed something silent or was out of ammunition for the more conventional weapons. His bow had a one-piece stock constructed from glass-filled polypropylene. His little monster was very lightweight but very, very rugged.

The stock had a thumb-hole pistol grip, giving Bee the appearance of a medieval gangster when wielding the thing. The prod was made of steel and could be left strong for long periods of time without placing undue stress upon it, thus making the bow desirable for drawn-out combat situations. The bow came equipped with a mounted, high-power scope. It had a 150-pound draw and shot eight-inch arrows. Depending on his mood, Bee could either use the arrows "straight" or have them coated with various chemical substances to maximize their effectiveness.

He glanced at the young men around him. They were good. Maybe excellent. But he knew they never would have survived long in the big "police action" in Nam.

They had to get down and get dirty *fast*.

If this outfit made it to Scotland, he'd be proud to teach them. After all, that's what he always wanted to be. A teacher.

Bee knew he had to use the bow and the shuriken effectively. After every kill, he'd have to retrieve the projectiles. He wasn't counting on finding a lot of replacement parts in Scotland.

Buddha Chan, after polishing his glasses, cleaned his M-21 a fourth time.

Freddie Mamudi ignored his M-16 and, instead, polished his pride and joy; his eclectic collection of knives. The V-42 stiletto. The Steele/Randel fighting knife. The Al Mar/Uzan Oda SHIVA fighting knife. And, for good measure, his traditional Chinese double knives. His double-horn Poignards, the double-short "Gim," and two Butterfly knives.

Mamudi stared at the Atlantic below him. He was an orphan, yet somehow he felt that wherever there was water, there would be a home for him, a Navy SEAL.

Kinski surveyed his weaponry. An Armalite AR-180 light assault rifle. Smaller, lighter and less accurate than a heavy assault rifle, with an effective range of 150 yards, it served him well for fighting on the run.

His treasured AK-47.

A Colt Government Model Mark IV .45 caliber automatic pistol. Kept in a holster located around his back, the modified pistol allowed him to stress his opinions effectively at close range. And in a world where any pack of fools would slit your throat for a carton of cigarettes, Kinski felt a kinship to his Colt.

A Remington 870 pump-action 12 gauge riot shotgun sat between his legs. It wasn't the greatest in terms of accuracy, but the shotgun was Kinski's key weapon when wandering around unpatrolled zones. You didn't have to hit a target with this gun so much as disintegrate it.

Crazy Jack just stared out the window. Below the plane was nothing but dark sea. He really didn't give a good goddamn what weapon he wound up with. It would do.

He had learned to survive no matter what the circumstances, and, in truth, he felt outside any battle he was thrust into. The only aspect of his life that had ever mattered to him, his family, had been obliterated during the last war, and now he was simply one small cog in a universe he no longer understood . . . hopefully a cog with a purpose. His training in New Age Physics helped him distance himself even farther from the mainstream.

He supposed that some people would call his mental processes Zoning Out. He didn't give a rat's ass. To Crazy Jack it was just a matter of surviving without cracking up. Every person had his own universe, he reckoned. Each individual universe contained an indefinite number of *other* universes with all variations and all other possibilities.

All things were happening all the time. There was no past, present or future in Jack's world. Everythig was *now*. All time was happening *now* . . . all history, past, present and future was happening *now*. It was just a matter of what plane, what time line you were on.

Crazy Jack hoped that on some other plane, on some other line of experience, his family was still living. Still happy. On some other level the last war never happened. That thought was the only one that gave solace to Crazy Jack. The idea that his family had escaped the horror that he had remained behind to endure. If that were the case, and, for Crazy Jack, that *had* to be the case . . . well, then, his life wasn't so empty after all.

His family hadn't died.

They had just shifted planes.

And he hadn't survived . . . he had simply been left behind, to make sure that the idiocy, the horror of this plane didn't *ever* lap over to infect another.

"Thinking hard?" MacGregor said, walking up to Crazy Jack in the pink cabin.

"Yeah." Jack nodded. "I suppose so."

"Once we land . . . do you have a weapon of choice?"

"You give me something, I'll shoot it, from a Thompson to a twenty-two. I'll be fine."

"I know you will."

MacGregor grinned at Jack. "You're going to love Scotland, you know. I can tell."

Jack stared at the darkness below. "I hope so. What kind of place is it? Most of the places I've been dumped into have been real boonie joints. Jungles so hot your sweat evaporated before it got to the top of your pores."

"Oh, Scotland is different from that," MacGregor said. "It's a dark place, but brilliant green. I tell you, Jack, it's a bonnie land. All the types of earth you can imagine in one small country. Some places are hot and barren. Other places are cold and snowy. But no matter what the spot, where the location, for at least half of the year, all you have is green, Jack. So many shades of green. And now that it's summer, it'll be misty. Foggy, but bonnie."

MacGregor eased himself back into the jet's chair. "God. I never appreciated that. You can look out at the Highlands and see ten shades of green on one hill. *Ten*, Jack. And sheep, just wandering around. Rams. Goats. Cows, with their bells clanging as they roam around.

"And the people? How they love the land. They don't want any big cities. They don't want skyscrapers. They still live in little flats and cottages, some made of stone, some two hundred years old and more. And everyone has a garden, Jack. No matter if the house is vast and huge or whether it's a teeny flat. They have flowers growing; whether it be in a land-scaped garden or a windowsill or a slice of backyard that's no more than one foot by two."

MacGregor's ruddy face grew pale. "Since the war, though, the country has changed. It's still like that, after a fashion. The green is still there, but the luster is gone. The sheep still wander, but they're ulcerated. Rams cling to the rocky hillsides, but they seldom get up. The goats don't jump from stone to stone, they shamble. And the cowbells still ring, but the cows give milk that's bloody red.

"The gardens are still there, as well, but the flowers are colorless, the ground sandy. The growings twisted and gnarled. Frightening, they are."

Crazy Jack stared at MacGregor. "It's like your whole life's been pulled out from under you, isn't it?"

MacGregor nodded. "Indeed it is. And I know you understand. I looked a little further into your files." He hesitated. "I'm sorry about your family."

"I am too, Mac." Crazy Jack sighed. "I am too."

"Well," MacGregor exhaled, slapping Jack on the back, "with your red hair and your fine, strapping spirit, I'm sure you'll find a fine extended family in Scotland."

Jack chuckled, staring at the moonlit sea below the plane. "I hope so, Mac. I'm getting a little old for all this shit."

Mac nodded. "Me too. Well, no matter. We'll be landing in Edinburgh in five minutes. A group of my villagers will be there to meet us with whatever arms they might have scavenged from the locals. We'll have time to think and plan and plot."

The plane suddenly rocked with an unprecedented violence. The pitch black view beneath exploded in a volcanic, fiery red.

"What the hell?" Kinski exclaimed.

"Looks that way," Crazy Jack deadpanned, staring at the seemingly molten action below the plane.

"We're taking flak!" the Gold Buddha yelled.

"Nothing we can do about it." Tom Bee shrugged. "This isn't an F-16."

"Passion pink yet!" Freddie belched.

Tom Bee glanced out the window. "Firing low and wide. FNGs in the FSE," he grinned quietly. "Probably couldn't fire a SAM properly if their lives depended on it." He began fingering his shuriken. "And they do."

"Goddamn them to hell!" MacGregor roared, gazing down from one of the windows.

"What is it?" Crazy Jack asked as the plane pitched, almost going into a roll avoiding the groundfire.

"That inferno up ahead!" MacGregor said, seething. "That's Edinburgh's airport."

Crazy Jack nodded. "Any flat terrain nearby?"

"Nothing to speak of."

"How far to the sea?"

"The plane will never survive a ditch," MacGregor growled.

"Well, then," Buddha said, rubbing his bald head for good luck. "I suppose we have to land."

Crazy Jack offered a boyish grin to the rest of his comrades. "Boys," he said, "it looks like they know we're coming."

SEVEN

By the time the plane landed, Edinburgh's airport looked like the kind of place only Dante could love. Large, spiral shards of flame erupted from what was left of the hangars and terminals.

The FSE goons' assault on the airport actually worked to the Marauders' advantage. The green troops' total zeal to destroy anything in sight obscured their own vision. Thick, black blankets of smoke wafted across the misty night sky, allowing the plane to approach with cover.

The jet skidded to a stop, its young pilot sweating enough to start a major new tributary in the U.K. As soon as he landed, a stray shot splintered the cockpit windshield and penetrated his skull. He died instantly, unaware of the worse fate that might await him if he had disembarked.

MacGregor felt the plane shutter to a stop. "Pilot's dead," he muttered.

"How can you be sure?" Kinski asked.

"I know his family. He was a commercial pilot. He'd never land this slovenly if he could help it."

Crazy Jack ignored the inferno outside. "So now what?"

MacGregor sighed, picking up the only weapon he had aboard, a Sterling Mark 7 "pistol" used by the U.K. during

35

the Falklands war. "We either deplane or get blown up with the aircraft."

"What went wrong?" Chan asked.

"Pick something," MacGregor muttered, walking toward the emergency exit.

He kicked it open, then deployed a rubber sliding device. "Welcome to Scotland, gents," he said with a smirk, hitting the slide.

The rest of the men followed.

As they slid down the half-deflated tube, they saw wrecked vehicles smoldering on the runways. Trucks. Cars. Vans. Bodies sprawled on the macadam. At least three dozen people had been caught by surprise, slaughtered before they had a chance to turn back.

The Marauders and MacGregor barely had time to get their sense of direction before countless armed men charged. Clad both in British police and army uniforms (what did it matter these days, anyway?), the troops plunged toward the plane, their semiautomatic weapons blazing.

The Marauders hid behind the massive tires of the jet plane, their blood boiling.

"Hell of a welcome, MacGregor," Crazy Jack muttered.

"What can I tell you?" Mac said. "Things just haven't been the same around here since the last war."

Crazy Jack turned to Kinski. "Got anything you can spare?"

Kinski tossed Crazy Jack his Remington riot piece and smiled. "You don't plan very well, do you?"

Jack shrugged. "You know how it is when you're lost in the cosmos."

The invaders continued to run forward, firing their semis.

"I don't know about you," the rotund Buddha muttered, "but I'm getting sick of this shit."

The bald, rotund man stood and calmly walked out into the bullet spray, his M-21 spurting hot lead in short, lethal bursts. Three men went down.

"What the fuck, excuse me," Freddie Mamudi said, firing his M-16 with one arm and fingering his beloved knives with the others.

"Guess this is it." Crazy Jack grinned.

The men charged forward into the FSE offensive.

"Serpentine," Crazy Jack yelled. The Marauders and MacGregor split up, zigzagging their way through the wreckage of the airport, using anything for cover.

Battered vehicles.

Ruptured walls of concrete.

Kinski ducked and rolled along the tarmac, spraying the field with his AK-47. The only thing he had going for him was his athletic agility. He could squirm on any surface with the herky-jerky motion of a guppy tossed up onto the sand. He wriggled and squiggled, always keeping the gun trained on the surprised and awkward FSE troops.

MacGregor and Crazy Jack were more of the bullheaded type. Since there wasn't much ground cover available to them, they didn't seek any. MacGregor roared forward, shouting something in Gaelic, gritting his teeth and firing in what amounted to a suicide mission. He knew he'd be cut down. It was just a matter of when. He had nothing to live for but his country. And, right now, that seemed a fading idea.

Crazy Jack, however, was not going to see the other redheaded man die. Repeatedly pumping the Remington, he dissolved three FSE thugs before they could draw a bead on MacGregor. He stopped only once, to wipe bits of human debris from his sweating brow.

Tom Bee, on the other hand, sat with his back at the left front wheel of the plane.

He should have seen this coming. Glancing about him, he instinctively knew how the entire show went down. Resistance men nail down the airport. No sign of FSE troops. Then FSE sappers open up on the now-confident locals. Slaughter. Nothing but slaughter. Local boys running around like scared rabbits, surrounded by well-armed troops.

Tom Bee sighed. He had definitely stepped into a No. 10 situation.

The pits.

Still, he had seen this sort of shit go down before. He sat patiently and watched the show roll toward him, his best dinky-dau expression on his face. It had been a long time.

He shook his shoulder-length black hair off his neck.

Slowly removing his tiny steel stars, he waited until the FSE troops were within twenty-five meters before he acted. He threw the nine Ninja shuriken with deadly accuracy, knowing that in this kind of a firefight he'd have to rely on his comrades' fire and his own steely courage to be effective.

One, two, three, four, five of the stars sliced into the foreheads of advancing FSE men, cracking open their skulls with a resounding crunch. The other four stars embedded themselves into the throats of four more advancing idiots, causing their bodies to stop their charge with a dizzying halt. The soldiers quivered, their arms waving through the air helplessly. Their weapons dropped to the ground, while their throats spewed crimson red fonts of blood onto the harsh, black macadam.

When he had used up his shuriken, Bee slowly pulled out his crossbow and, shortly after loading the first time, shot a "British" commando clean through the right eye. He didn't wait to see the bits of brain smash through the man's head and splatter onto the runway. He had no time to gloat. Only time to reload.

Kinski ran forward, a man possessed. Remembering his homeland, Poland, and remembering who the suckers before him represented, he simply put his head down and, opening up with his AK-47, charged. It didn't matter to him whether the air around him was sizzling under the impact of semiautomatic fire. It didn't matter to him that he might be killed thousands of miles either from his real home or the home of his fathers. For Kinski, all that mattered was *this* mission. He had volunteered for it. It was his duty to see it through. "Rock and roll!" he bellowed, charging forward.

He trotted from the remains of one burning vehicle to another, keeping as low to the ground as possible.

Bullets thwacked into the blazing metal around him. Squinting his eyes to see through the smoke, he continued to send round after around at the FSE goons.

He didn't notice the bodies and the blood at his feet.

Mamudi, witnessing the dance of death for the very first time since the last big war, experienced a trance-like state. Bullets zipping all around him, he raised his wiry hands to the sky and, uttering a Muslim prayer, ignored the firepower and yanked out two Chinese blades. Using two figure-eight slash configurations, he danced through the stunned East German troops that now passed for British police, nicely slicing their necks and midsections. He stopped furtively a few times to jam a blade through their necks into their brains. His glass eye spattered with blood, its skull and cross-bones covered, he howled at the night sky and continued to thrust and parry.

In the confusion, with misfit soldiers battling the FSE men in a crazy-quilt manner, pandemonium broke loose. A jeep carrying four heavily armed FSE grunts, their .30 caliber machineguns blazing, pulled out onto the field.

The FSE hadn't expected much of a fight from the Marauders, so the men in the jeep were addled. Their guns spat out slugs at both FSE men and the Marauders alike.

Buddha Chan grinned.

The four men in the jeep were wearing grenade belts.

Standing up and taking careful aim, Buddha picked up his M-21 and aimed at one of the men's belts.

"The best sniper in the fucking corps," he whispered, squeezing off a round.

All action stopped.

The air itself seemed to ignite.

A roar smashed through the sky like a white, hot fist. What had been a vehicle was now a screaming, screeching fireball, careening across the airstrip.

Crazy Jack yelled, "Way to go, Buddha!"

He spotted MacGregor, his pistol empty, fighting off the FSE goons at close quarters with his studded fist. The burly Scot pounded several of the men into a state of semiconsciousness, lashing out at them with his leather-encased sputnik-hand.

His nostrils were filled with the smell of burning flesh. His legs bled, fragged by the explosions around him. He felt nothing. Only rage. Lash out, he willed himself, hit anything solid.

"Hold on, Mac!" Crazy Jack yelled, charging into the fray, one hand holding a combat knife, the other hand forming a massive fist.

Crazy Jack sensed the FSE goon before he saw him. The towering East European emerged from the black smoke separating Jack from MacGregor. His face charred beyond belief, the FSE lackey was running on sheer pain. He swung his AK-47 in Jack's direction.

Jack clutched his Marine-issue, Bowie-style K-bar. There

were three ways to kill a man quickly with a knife, he knew. He could strike between the fifth and sixth ribs with a rapid jam upward and a twist motion to puncture the heart. He could try to ram the knife below the charging giant's left ear, or he could try for number three.

Lunging through the air, he grabbed the burly invader around the neck, yanking his head back and slicing violently with the knife. Jack left the man convulsing behind him as he continued his tumblesault into the donnybrook MacGregor was staging for the benefit of a small group of FSE thugs.

Before long, the entire firefight was reduced to Jack and MacGregor punching one lone, muscular FSE man into a state resembling marmalade.

"I thank you for your help," MacGregor said.

"No problem," Crazy Jack wheezed. "It was about time I exercised this hand." He flexed his bruised left fist.

Silence engulfed the airfield.

Without uttering a word, Tom Bee retrieved his bloodied shuriken and steel arrows. He couldn't replace them in alien territory.

Freddie wiped the blood from his knives off on the legs of the dead. He then pulled out his blood-drenched glass eye. "Gonna be hell to clean off," he muttered.

Chan walked around the felled FSE troops, collecting weaponry. "Nice stuff," he muttered.

Kinski staggered back to the side of the plane. "Nice little country you have here, MacGregor," he gasped. "What do we take on next? The Loch Ness Monster?"

Crazy Jack stood next to MacGregor. "Looks like someone tipped the FSE off to our plans," he said.

MacGregor stared out at the battlefield where three dozen of his townspeople lay slaughtered. "Seems that way."

"Mac, it's your show," Crazy Jack shrugged.

"Gather whatever weapons we can carry, whatever ammunition," MacGregor muttered.

"Uh-huh," Crazy Jack grunted.

"Then . . . ," MacGregor said, rubbing the blood off his spiked hand, "let's get the hell out of here."

Jack shrugged. "Sounds like a good plan to me."

EIGHT

The six warriors slogged alongside the road leading to Edinburgh. It was a cold, dank night, and fog seemed to rise up from the land like tendrils, enveloping their feet, reaching for their lungs.

Tom Bee walked point.

The rotund Buddha played tail-end Charlie, carefully training his weapon at any sign of a rear assault. He didn't like this new land. It was too cold. Too damp. Too dark.

In the middle, MacGregor, Crazy Jack, Freddie Mamudi and Kinski padded through the damp underbrush. The night sky behind them was a vivid orange. Edinburgh's airport resembled Mount Vesuvius after a bad rumble.

"I don't mind telling you," Crazy Jack said, "this doesn't look too hot."

MacGregor nodded. "Treachery," he said. "Plain and simple."

Mamudi nudged Kinski. "Trouble coming."

Kinksi squinted his eyes, raising his AK-47. "Nope. It's Bee."

Tom Bee trotted over to the men. "FSE trops. Four klicks ahead."

"They must have seen the airport," MacGregor growled.

41

"It's not exactly something you can miss," Crazy Jack grinned.

"Want to try to take them out?" Kinski asked. "We have the firepower and the experience."

"Negative." Bee replied. "Kinski. Get the Buddha forward. We lay low."

Kinski nodded and ran into the darkness. Within a matter of seconds the rumble of engines could be heard slithering up the road. Kinski and Buddha Chan trotted up to their comrades just as the rest of the men flattened themselves against the cold, damp earth.

Two four-by-fours filled with FSE troops roared by. The troops were heavily armed and ready to fight.

"We could nail them," Kinski whispered.

"We could also leave a trail of dead bodies leading from here to Edinburgh," Bee hissed. "That would make it really hard for them to track us, wouldn't it?"

Kinski grunted by way of response.

The trucks thundered toward the flame-encased airport. Bee slowly got to his feet. "Come on," he said. "We're not far from Edinburgh. I saw the lights up ahead."

MacGregor straightened his massive frame. "I just hope there's someone there waiting for us . . . someone not with the FSE."

The men trudged for another half hour before they found themselves sprawled face down in the dirt again. A pickup truck loaded with wheat chugged up the road.

"We could use that truck," Kinski offered.

"That's the truth," MacGregor said, "but if it's a local boy, I'd rather we take it without any blood spilled. You all lay low. I'll see what the situation is."

"It could be a trap," Freddie hissed.

"It could," MacGregor replied. "But even if it is, a Scot looks a lot more at home in these parts than a Muslim from Afghanistan."

Freddie smirked. "Good point."

"And a one-eyed one at that," MacGregor said.

Leaving his weapon behind, MacGregor stepped out into the road. Bathed in the glare of the headlights, the massive Scot waved his injured fist, flagging down the truck.

The driver, clad in a bulky cap and overcoat, sent the truck stuttering to a stop. "Excuse me," MacGregor said, ever the gentleman. "My car broke down up ahead, and I was wondering if you'd be so kind as to give me a lift back to town?"

The driver smiled and removed the hat. A headful of glistening brown hair tumbled down. "I could." She smiled.

"A lassie!" MacGregor gasped. "What are you doing driving a produce truck so late at night? It's dangerous out here."

"Things are tough all over," she said. "What's the matter with your hand?"

"I, uh, injured it."

"It looks shattered," she said, emphasizing the last word. MacGregor nodded. "That it is."

"Shatterhand," she said flatly.

MacGregor stiffened. Only the locals in the resistance knew him by that name. It was now or never. He nodded his head, half expecting to catch a slug between the eyes. "Some call me that."

"Good," she said. "Tell your friends to come out of hiding and get the hell in the truck as fast as their legs can carry them."

MacGregor nodded to the three men in the underbrush. Bee and Chan closed in on the truck from the opposite direction.

"A woman!" Freddie smiled.

"Very observant," the woman said, not looking at the gleam in Mamudi's eye. "Get in the back. There's a wooden compartment beneath the top layer of grain. You won't be seen. And hurry it up a bit, will you? The place is crawling with FSE slime."

"But the troops," Crazy Jack began, "won't they stop you?"

"Mister," the woman replied, "food is a scarcity in these parts. Nobody in their right mind would stop a truck filled with grain from entering Edinburgh."

The man trotted to the back of the truck. Kinski reached in beneath the outer layer of grain, carefully arranged to look like a truckload. Beneath a blanket was a hatch. He flicked it and lifted it open. The back of the truck had been converted into a large cargo hold, big enough to hold ammo, supplies or men.

Kinski grinned and slithered into the hold. The other men followed. MacGregor was the last to climb inside.

"Are there still Freedom Fighters left in Edinburgh?" he asked.

"You're looking at one," the woman replied.

"Where are you headquartered?"

"The only place the FSE slime won't look for us. The Castle."

MacGregor smiled, enjoying the irony of that, and climbed inside, slamming the latch behind him.

The woman, grinding gears, hung a drastic U-turn on the road and drove slowly but surely toward the city of Edinburgh. She allowed the two four-by-fours filled with cursing FSE troops to roar past her, returning from a very disappointing visit to the Edinburgh airport.

The men in the hold stared out at the city of Edinburgh through the weapon slats of the walls. The city was both new and ancient; it had originated back in the sixth century as a hill fort and had continually modernized until shortly before the last war.

This evening its streets were deserted but for the occasional FSE patrol.

For the Marauders, who had never seen much of the world outside the States except dangerous fighting terrain, the sight of the pristine city was awe-inspiring.

The New Town, with its classical Georgian streets and elegant tree-lined squares, seemed untouched by the FSE goons.

This was a lie, they all knew. Behind the facades that once housed banks, stately private homes and government buildings now lurked schemers in the employ of Maximov.

The truck rumbled onward through the Old Town. With its close medieval architecture and narrow, winding streets, it seemed to have been lifted from a book of fairy tales. There were pubs in the area that were four hundred years old. Now they catered, not to the locals, but to the invading hordes.

The truck passed the Prince's Street gardens, where old gravestones mingled with newly constructed FSE barracks.

The men lurched in the cargo hold as the truck began the long incline to the Castle. There had been some kind of fortress structure in place in Edinburgh since 600 A.D., towering above the surrounding area on its great rock. In medieval times it was even a royal residence. Before the war it was largely a tourist trap, with its military museum and its royal jewels. After the invasion the FSE troops promptly looted the place, destroying most of its historic value. Yet still it stood, proud and strong, high above the city. The perfect vantage point to spot FSE troops.

Also, the perfect place to be spotted by FSE troops.

Still, if the locals trusted the spot, the Marauders had to.

The men in the truck felt the vehicle lurch to a halt. Led by MacGregor, they clambered out the back of the cargo hold. The woman, ignoring the Marauders, motioned to Mac-Gregor. The men shambled across to the high walls of the ancient castle, assembling in what had once been the monument to Scotland's military men killed in battle over the years.

With large, carved plaques honoring the dead suspended eerily on the walls, the Marauders entered the massive structure, greeted by the faces of a hundred stone-faced men.

The young woman walked over to the men. "Gentlemen, this is Shatterhand MacGregor and his *friends*."

MacGregor nodded at the assembled.

" 'Tis a sad day, Katt," a bald, bearded man nodded at the woman. "Yet one of hope, too."

The old man stood up and shook MacGregor's good hand. "On behalf of the men of Edinburgh, I, Liam McBride, welcome you and your fellow patriots."

MacGregor nodded by way of thanks.

The old man smiled. "You've already met Katt Shea."

"Not formally," Freddie Mamudi said, grinning.

The old man ignored Freddie, concentrating on Mac-Gregor. "She's our leader now. Her father, a fine soul, perished not a week ago at the hands of the FSE assassins."

"I'm sorry." MacGregor blanched. "I didn't know."

"He died for a cause," Katt Shea said. "It was good enough for him and good enough for me. Now sit down. All of you. We have a lot of planning to do."

The Marauders sat down as the brown-haired girl paced back and forth in the great hall of the dead. Mamudi couldn't help noticing that she was shapely. Wonderfully so. Twenty-five years of age, no more. Round breasts encased beneath a flannel shirt. Bluejeans clinging to her body. Old-fashioned boots extending to mid-calf. Mamudi sighed. He'd be proud to take her as a wife.

"What exactly went down at the airport?" Crazy Jack asked.

Shea faced the man. "All hell broke loose."

"*That* I knew," Crazy Jack said.

Shea fumed at him. "Then why ask me stupid questions?"

"Excuse me, miss," Tom Bee said, flints of steel appearing in his eyes. "His question wasn't stupid. I appreciate your situation. This is your country. But you must appreciate ours. We came here to help. We arrived. Everything was fugazi."

The young, white-skinned girl blinked. "Fugazi?"

"All fucked up," Bee said, not blinking.

Katt Shea burst out into a laugh. "Welcome to the real world, Mr. . . ."

"Bee," Tom said. "How bad are things?"

Shea leaned against a monument, blushing. "Pretty bad, and, then again, not so. I'm not sure where to begin."

"At the beginning, lassie," MacGregor said.

"We knew of your arrival," Katt breathed. "We have an informant in London. Very highly placed."

"His name?" Buddha Chan asked.

"We don't know," Katt said. "We call him 'Montrose.' Part of our history, you see."

"I understand," The rotund Buddha said, polishing his glasses. "It would be lost on me."

"I'm sorry," Katt replied. "That wasn't a snub. Montrose told us of your change in plans—arriving in Edinburgh instead of London. We rallied what support we could muster on two hours' notice. They went to the airport."

"And were slaughtered," Crazy Jack said.

"And were *slaughtered*," Katt repeated angrily. "It would seem, gentlemen, that someone knows everything we do *before* we do it."

"Not the cheeriest of prospects," Kinski said.

"Nope," Freddie said, still rolling his good eye in Katt's direction. "But we're here now. We can change all that."

MacGregor frowned. "It might not be as easy as that. If we have a mole in the ranks, it could wreak havoc with our plans."

He turned to Katt. "Who do we have left? "

Katt smiled. "Here are the pluses and the minuses. We have every veteran member of the infantry, especially the Queen's Own Highlanders, the Black Watch, the Gordon Highlanders and Argyll and Sutherland Highlanders. Royal Scots? They're still proud of being the oldest infantry in the British army.

"On the downside, the FSE has pushed everyone way underground. They have the weaponry. We have whatever we can salvage. They are better armed but still wet behind the ears when it comes to our turf. We aren't seasoned but we're scrambling.''

MacGregor massaged his eyelids. ''What about the clans?''

''We've sent pointers to the Highlands and Northwestern Highlands. It'll be risky, because most of the clansmen have gone underground as well. They have a better chance of being ignored by the FSE up there because of the terrain.''

''What about the terrain?'' Buddha asked.

''Using American slang, gentlemen,'' Katt smiled sweetly, ''it sucks. It's hard to get to. It switches from green to dead rockface within a matter of miles, and you have to be either a masochist or a mountain goat to want to live there . . . that's why we love it.''

''Understood,'' Buddha said, replacing his glasses on the bridge of his nose.

''This is what we know . . . ,'' Katt continued.

''Via Montrose?'' Crazy Jack ventured.

''Via Montrose.'' Katt nodded. ''The FSE is shipping in troops through London en masse. They plan to congregate at Aberdeen and launch a massive fleet of small, piddly boats toward the North Sea.''

''The oil rigs,'' Freddie muttered.

''Of *course*, the oil rigs,'' Katt spat. ''Did ya think they were heading off for a picnic?''

Crazy Jack raised his massive paw. ''I know I'll sound ignorant about all this, but exactly *how* important are the rigs to the FSE?''

Katt ran a lean hand through her long brown hair. ''Plenty and moreso. Since 1970, when oil was discovered in the North Sea off Aberdeen, the rigs have crawled toward the Shetland Islands. They've virtually bolstered the Brits' economy from their construction until the last war. It is, gentlemen, the *only* source of fuel in the United Kingdom, aside from the nuclear reactors, and you can't make fighter planes fly with nuclear energy, if you catch my drift.''

Buddha Chan nodded, massaging his round, bald head. ''So it seems that it's up to us to turn the situation around.''

''You'll have plenty of help.'' Katt added, ''I hope.''

Tom Bee stood, his granite jaw grinding his teeth. ''What have your people worked out?'' he asked.

''We're not used to fighting our allies,'' Katt said, a slight smile on her face. "At least, not in the last two hundred years or so. But we figure that the FSE British troops will cut a path up to Aberdeen the conventional way. By road."

"So how do we beat them?" Bee asked.

"A two-pronged offensive," Katt said. "One, by road. The second, by rail."

Bee smiled. The woman had both beauty and brains.

Katt continued. "We, the Lowlanders, will take the road toward Aberdeen. You" —she nodded toward MacGregor— "will have to take the rail to the Highlands, rally the clans and then meet up with us in the city."

"Won't the rail be dangerous?" MacGregor asked.

"I hope not," Katt replied. "It's regularly used by what's left of British Rail to ship supplies to the FSE louts north. What you, what *we*, have to do is purloin a train and send it to Highland country. It shouldn't be too hard. We have supporters all along the trail. They can switch tracks accordingly. Most of the tracks leading to the Highlands haven't been used since before the war. There's not a great deal of tourist activity heading to the Highlands today."

MacGregor nodded. "Where are the clans supposed to gather?"

"Inverness," the woman replied.

"Wuzzat?" Crazy Jack asked.

"It's a wee town that's known as the capital of the Highlands," MacGregor replied. "It's not far from Drommoise Muir. That was the last battle site fought by the Scots on British soil, the Battle of Culloden. It was there the clansmen of Bonnie Prince Charlie were crushed by George II's redcoats. It won't be hard to get to."

Kinski frowned. "The part of all this I don't understand," he ventured, "is how we manage to get there by rail. So far we haven't had a lot of luck with secrecy. It's not like we can just walk into the train station and say, 'Excuse me, may we borrow one of your trains?' I mean, I wouldn't mind trying that. I've talked my way out of worse situations but . . .'"

"There's an old train in Edinburgh station," Katt replied. "*The Royal Scotsman*. In the days before the war it was a luxury train. A one-hundred-year-old beauty used by tourists. We simply *borrow* it. It hasn't been used since the FSE took over. They probably don't even know it exists. It's been lying dormant. Mothballed.''

"But surely the FSE troops will see it pull out," Crazy Jack said.

"Not if there's something else occupying their time," Katt answered.

"Such as?" Crazy Jack asked.

"Such as a horrible explosion that will . . . that will *destroy* Edinburgh Castle."

Silence engulfed the room.

"You have the manpower and firepower to do that?" Mamudi asked.

"That we have," Katt nodded.

"Then, I suppose," Mamudi replied, "that we best do as the lady—er, lassie—says. It's her territory."

The Marauders nodded.

Crazy Jack stood and walked across the room toward the memorial for the nurses who died during World War II. "Here's what I suggest. Two of us should go with Katt and her troops toward Aberdeen by road. The rest of us into the Highlands to meet the clans."

"Sounds good," Tom Bee nodded.

"I'll volunteer to go with Miss Shea," Mamudi said, grinning.

"I'll go as well," Tom Bee said.

"Perhaps only *one* of us should accompany the lady," Mamudi said.

"I think everyone would be safer with two escorts." Crazy Jack replied.

"Then it's settled." MacGregor nodded. "I will go with the rest of you into the Highlands."

Buddha Chan sat beneath a monument to the King's Own Scottish Borders and sighed. "You know what I like about this mission?"

Kinski ran a comb through his hair. "What?"

"The advanced military tactics."

Kinski laughed, combing his blond pompadour into a near spiral. "Picky, picky, picky."

Buddha Chan was forced to laugh. But it was hollow laughter.

NINE

The following morning MacGregor and Katt decided the time was right to venture into the town to alert the locals that help was at hand. Crazy Jack would go along as proof of America's support and would try to pass as a local, owing to his red hair.

The rest of the Marauders weren't all that enthused about the plan, but since they were aliens, they agreed to go along with it.

The Royal Pub would be the meeting place, since the oldest denizens of the town would be congregating there.

Come noon, the threesome set out as inconspicuously as possible in a town overrun by FSE goons.

They strolled along the narrow streets to the pub located in the Old Town.

"Did you know that Robert Louis Stevenson based his *Jekyll and Hyde* on a character who lived here?" Katt muttered as she strolled past the heavily armed guards.

"No," Crazy Jack replied.

"Well, he did," Katt said. "He was a reverend. He preached by day and went around murdering by night. Stevenson's mother told him the story when he was a lad, and when he was an adult, he expanded upon it."

"Now, why doesn't that make me feel more relaxed?" Crazy Jack replied, glancing at the sallow faces of the FSE troops patrolling the area.

50

"Calm down, Yank," MacGregor whispered. "You're amongst friends here."

"Right," Crazy Jack said.

The threesome entered the old pub. Inside, fifty or more pale-faced, weary Scots sat in near silence. They were drinking early. They drank to forget the past. But most of all, they drank to forget the present and the future.

Katt led them to a table for three. "Three pints o'bitters," she said to the barkeep.

"Aye," he responded.

An old man, named McClennen, staggered up to the table. "So, how goes it, Katt?"

"Sit down, McClennen," she told the stout, bearded fellow. The man, who more than resembled Santa Claus, lurched down into a seat.

"This," Katt said, "is a fella named Crazy Jack. He's from America. He's come to help us."

McClennen snorted. "America hasn't seen fit to help us thus far."

Crazy Jack nodded. "We've had troubles of our own."

McClennen grinned into his lager. "I doubt it. America is a rich country, a big country. You probably escaped most of the troubles of the last war."

Crazy Jack bridled. "Well, let me tell you something, *Scot*. A lot of us didn't miss our share of troubles. A lot of us fared worse than you'll ever imagine."

McClennen snorted. MacGregor put a protective hand on Jack's arm. "Jack, we're here to make friends."

"I have all the friends I need," Jack said, his blue eyes flashing. He faced the bearded McClennen. "I had a wife, Debra. And two kids, Jack and Jillian. They lived in New Jersey. It's a state in America."

"I know that," McClennen said.

"Well . . . , I lost them," Crazy Jack stated. "And I don't know how they died. I can only imagine. Maybe Debra had gotten up one morning to get the kids up for school. I was in the service, so I wasn't there.

"Maybe she made them wash up. Maybe she scolded them for being late for the school bus. The kids could have come downstairs for breakfast, sulking. Maybe she gave them cold cereal and they didn't like it. Maybe she made them their favorite, flapjacks with maple syrup. I don't know for sure.

"I don't know if the kids ever got out of the house before the first bombs hit the oil refineries nearby. But I damn sure know what the result was. A sudden flash.

"A startled look. A blast of light. I don't know who would have screamed first . . . probably the kids. My wife would try to grab them, snatch them closer, protect them like any parent would. But there was no protecting them from *this*. She shut her eyes. The light would invade her anyway. Clear through the eyelids. Maybe the kids were hugging her, holding onto her tighter. And then, what?

"A wave of heat and dust. They'd be seared, my friend. Pulverized into ash. Slammed against the side of my home . . . if my home was left standing.

"Maybe they'd whimper. Maybe they'd cry as their bodies were reduced to an ashen silhouette against whatever wall of the house was left. Maybe they'd be a shadow for a nanosecond before the house itself blew away."

. Crazy Jack paused, running a massive hand through his orange locks. "I can't say. You see, that whole area of the country is still too *hot* to enter. If you're stupid enough to try, you die. The radiation eats through your skin and gets to your bones. You breathe it. You cough it. You cry it. You shit it. It'll be a hot spot for years to come, my friend. So I can't go there to find out what happened to my family. Three people whose biggest crime was being in the wrong place at the wrong time."

He stared at McClennen. "So don't *ever* question why I'm here. What I've gone through, you'll never know. Yet I'm still standing. Still fighting. I'm here to help you. That's all that should matter to you. Not whether I'm from a country that's big, or a country that was rich or another fucking planet."

The portly, bearded Scot named McClennen bowed his head. "I'm sorry for your family, son."

"That makes two of us," Crazy Jack replied. "Now, if you're with Katt, you're with me and my kind. We have to knock out the FSE, and we have to knock them out *fast*. What do you have by way of manpower?"

McClennen looked up furtively. "Five hundred seasoned troops, son. Badly armed, but ready to fight. We want to march into Aberdeen. We want to keep the bastards from growing stronger. We may pick up others on the way, but we can't be sure of that.''

"Fine." Crazy Jack replied. "We're here to help you in every way we can."

"How thick are the FSE troops in these parts?" MacGregor asked.

"Thicker than honey and getting thicker." McClennen replied. "The FSE boys seem to have our resistance pegged solid. They found out you were arriving before *we* did, and they *wiped out* anyone they thought was helping ye."

"My village?" MacGregor began.

"Gone," McClennen said. "In a fireball."

"Was it fast?" MacGregor asked.

The Santa Claus-looking man blanched. "I'd be lying to you if I said so."

MacGregor pounded his studded fist into the table.

McClennen stared at his knuckles. "First, they stormed in. They took the women and did what they wanted with them before killing them."

"Double veterans," Crazy Jack growled.

"What?" Katt asked.

"In old times," he replied, "those were guys who screwed somebody and then killed her."

MacGregor clutched his shattered fist with his good hand. "And then?"

"Then," McClennen continued, "they took the children and well, you know . . ."

"Slaughtered them," MacGregor finished.

"The men were tortured. They didn't know too much about our operation, so, for the most part, they were killed for sport after the FSE bastards discovered that there wasn't much knowledge to glean," McClennen said.

MacGregor nodded. "Nothing left?"

"They torched the houses," McClennen said. "Lobbed in a few grenades for good measure. They wanted to see the debris fly."

"So I have nothing?" MacGregor asked.

"Nothing to go home to," McClennen finished.

"Christ," MacGregor hissed, "what's it worth?"

"It's damned worth fighting for," Crazy Jack said, pounding his fist on the table. "You have the chance I never had.

Your country isn't wiped out. Your people aren't scattered, fragmented, stunned. *Now* is the time to rise up."

Katt smiled. "Spoken like a true, hot-headed American."

"I'm all you've got, little sister," Crazy Jack grinned. "Make the most of it."

McClennen offered a smile beneath his white beard. "Then it's on to Aberdeen?"

MacGregor nodded. "That it is."

"The locals are ready," McClennen said. "As are all the locals on the way. We've sent runners. We've let them all know you're here."

"And we have plans," Crazy Jack said. "Plans to make the FSE crazy. We have to be well coordinated and we have to be strong. We have to hit the fuckers fast and *hard*."

McClennen grinned. "You wouldn't be a true Scot, would ya?"

Crazy Jack returned the smile. "Let's just say I'm a citizen of the new free world."

"That's good enough for me, Yank," McClennen said. "Quick now, dummy up and pretend to be soused."

"Why?"

"It seems that your presence here is known. At the door. FSE. Honcho. Nahaczewski."

A thin, sallow man strode into the pub, followed by two broad-shouldered goons.

MacGregor leaned forward. "Major military?"

"*The* major military," McClennen uttered.

Nahaczewski marched up to the bar. "Lager," he demanded, his reedy voice snapping like a bullwhip. "Dark."

The rotund bartender brought him a glass. The reptilian man picked it up and swallowed it in a demonstration of kidney power. He slammed the empty glass onto the bar and turned to the denizens of the pub.

"Quite a few of our local law enforcement officers were killed last night," he announced.

The pub offered a collective "Awwww!"

The thin man with the face of a python stared at the gathering. "I don't suppose anyone here would know anything about it."

The innocent pub-goers shook their heads.

The serpent grinned evilly, "I didn't think as much."

With his two goons in tow, the snake marched around the

pub, singling out different denizens. "*You*? I didn't think so. And *you*? No, I'd think not."

He walked up to Katt and smiled. "But *you*," he said, practically drooling onto her ample breasts. "Perhaps I'd better take *you* into custody . . . for questioning. Long, intensive questioning. Perhaps after a few hours or a few days we could come to an *understanding*."

Katt stared the man down. "I doubt it."

The snake's two goons moved forward. MacGregor didn't budge. Crazy Jack couldn't believe it.

The two goons dragged Katt out of her seat.

"I know you will enjoy the time we spend together." The FSE slime smiled.

Katt didn't respond.

Crazy Jack, enraged, leaped to his feet. "She wouldn't," he declared, "but I know *I* would."

MacGregor moaned.

Katt sighed.

Nahaczewski glared at the man. "And *who*, may I ask, are *you*?"

"Jack," the red-headed man sputtered. "Jack . . . *MacKowen*."

McClennen sank low into his chair.

"I haven't seen you before," the FSE man said.

"You haven't been looking very hard," Jack replied.

"That isn't a Scottish accent, is it?" the snake asked.

"How would you know?" Jack said sweetly. "I believe that's a Ukrainian lilt I detect in your voice."

Nahaczewski began to boil. "And what makes you so certain of that fact?"

Crazy Jack grinned. "I traveled a bit before the war, and wouldn't you know it? I wound up spending time behind the Iron Curtain. It's a lovely place, if you don't mind the *stink* from the government buildings."

The snake began to simmer. "Where did your travels take you?"

"Beyond your wildest dreams," Crazy Jack answered.

"Take him! *And the girl*!" the snake hissed.

Crazy Jack flexed his massive chest. "I don't think so, slimeball." ·

MacGregor sank lower in his seat. "Now, *now*, Jack."

But Jack was already in action. The first thug came at him,

fists flying. Jack grinned and reached a massive hand below the burly hulk's groin. Grabbing onto his testicles hard, he lifted the screaming man up and sent him flying twenty feet across the pub into a solid oak wall. "Two points for the birth control team," Jack muttered.

The groaning goon staggered to his feet and, clutching his vital parts, charged Jack.

Jack easily got out of the way, karate-chopping the moron on the back of the neck. The man went down on the floor. This time he wasn't moaning.

"The boy doesn't seem too well," Jack told the FSE honcho. "Maybe you'd better take him home."

The second goon leaped through the air like a champion wrestler playing ballet star. Jack didn't have to think twice. Grabbing the curly-headed East European by his hair, he yanked the boy back, mid-flight, effectively breaking his neck and sending him slamming down onto the sawdust floor.

"Hulk Hogan you're not," he spat.

Crazy Jack stood before the stunned crowd, facing the reptile named Nahaczewski. "Now, I believe you were saying something about the young lady and myself?"

The snake pulled a .45 and aimed it at Jack. "*I* am the authority here," he wheezed.

"Nope," Jack said, still smiling. "You *were* the authority here."

Jack advanced slowly toward the quivering bag of bones. "My name is Jack Keenan. I am six feet four inches tall and weigh 230 pounds."

The snake fired blindly. Jack easily dodged the slug. He continued his litany. "I'm a former Green Beret captain. I'm a West Point graduate."

A second bullet whizzed by his head.

"I did three tours in Nicaragua."

Bang. Zing.

"My mother's name was McCarthy. My father's name was Kennaczeswki. . . . You and your kind drove my father away from his homeland. He died in poverty."

Bang. Whizzz.

Katt and MacGregor watched helplessly as red-haired, blue-eyed Crazy Jack Keenan advanced on the man like a grizzly bear gone wild.

Nahaczewski tried to get off another shot. Crazy Jack didn't allow that, however. He wrapped a massive left paw around the sallow, puny FSE man's hand, effectively crunching all the bones. The man screamed as the gun fell to the ground.

Crazy Jack lifted the man high into the air, and placing his knee firm on a solid oak table, brough the man slamming down across it.

Crunch.

The room winced as the FSE man howled.

Crazy Jack glared down at the man as he heard the fellow's spine crack in two.

The man went limp in his arms.

He allowed him to flop onto the floor.

Crazy Jack, sweating, steaming, stared down at the flapping, flopping carcass. "I am Ukrainian," he said. "You took my homeland. You took my father's family away from him. I am Crazy Jack Keenan. I am six feet four inches tall and weigh 230 pounds. I am a former Green Beret captain. A West Point graduate. I did three tours in Nicaragua, you sonofabitch bastard."

The FSE man writhed, screeching in a high-pitched wail, on the floor.

MacGregor ran up to Jack. "We'd better go."

Jack shook himself out of his stupor. "What? Say what?"

Katt shook his left arm. "Jack, we have to get back to the others."

Jack nodded dumbly, catching a glimpse of a smiling McClennen. "Show's you how the Yanks are on your side, eh, sport?" He grinned, more than slightly embarrassed at his emotional outbreak.

McClennen nodded, rubbing a gnarled hand across his white beard.

Before Jack could move, the air around him was filled with the sounds of sirens and whistles.

The FSE were on the alert.

Jack stood granitelike in the middle of the pub.

"Christ," MacGregor shouted. "It's the law!"

"We're done for," Katt moaned.

"No," Jack said. "You go and join the others. I'll get by."

"Are you daft, man?" Katt asked.

"No." Jack smiled sadly. "Just realistic."

"What are you talking about?" Katt demanded.

"It's not the individuals that count, miss. It's the mission.

You and Mac get out of here. This is all my fault. I'll stand on my own."

"You're crazy," MacGregor growled.

"So they say." Jack smiled. He turned to the white-haired, bearded man. "Tell them, McClennen. You're old enough to know what's what."

The Santa Claus man nodded. "He's right. You two get out of here. The mission will continue. As for your friend here, we'll do the best we can for him. Now *go*."

Crazy Jack smiled. "You heard the man. Get the fuck out of here. I'll do fine."

MacGregor and Katt trotted toward a back entrance, turning one last time toward Jack and all the men in the pub. "Tonight," MacGregor bellowed. "We leave tonight."

"Aye," the men in the pub grunted.

There was a commotion at the front door.

MacGregor and Katt slipped out the back way.

Within seconds a group of FSE goons in uniform burst into the pub. "We heard there was trouble," one of them announced.

No one in the pub spoke. Crazy Jack Keenan stepped forward. "No trouble," he said firmly.

The head FSE goon looked toward the floor. Two of his comrades were dead. One would never diddle again.

"What do you call this?" he demanded.

Jack grinned. "Darwinism at its finest."

The members of the pub applauded.

One of the troops caught a glimpse of Nahaczewski, his body twisted like a discarded rag doll. "What happened?" the soldier demanded.

"Break dancing can be dangerous to your health." Jack said solemnly.

The FSE slime rushed toward Crazy Jack Keenan. He didn't resist. He was handcuffed and shackled. The nondescript FSE mob led him out of the pub into the harsh sunlight of an occupied day in Scotland.

Before leaving the pub, he turned to the clientele and winked.

Fifty men winked back at him.

As Jack was led from the pub, he realized that the mission would go on no matter what his fate.

That wouldn't make what awaited him any less painful.

But it would make the ordeal worth something.

TEN

"He *what*?" Tom Bee exclaimed.

"For the upteenth time," MacGregor said, "he creamed two of them and just about broke a third in two."

"Great," Bee muttered. "Excellent. Well thought out. Wonderfully disciplined."

"He saved my life," Katt emphasized.

"He jeopardized the entire mission," Bee said flatly.

"Not so," MacGregor said. "If anything convinced the townspeople that you Yanks were on our side, it was Jack's action."

"Besides," Mamudi offered, "he was defending a lady's virtue."

"Quite nicely," Buddha Chan added. "You think he broke the main man's back?"

"At least," MacGregor said. "Maybe snapped it into threesomes."

Buddha rubbed his head. "Nice move. Good hands."

Kinski sat in the corner of the monument room at the Castle. "So how does this affect us?"

"It doesn't," Bee said. "We leave tonight, by rail, as planned."

"We can't leave Jack in prison," Mamudi declared. "It isn't *honorable*."

"So," Bee said, "what do you suggest?"

Mamudi lapsed into silence. He didn't really know.

Kinski produced a pocket comb and proceeded to attend to his Fabian haircut. "Well," he said, "we were planning on creating a disturbance anyhow. Why not blow up the prison as well as the Castle? On our way to the train station, I mean."

"Sounds like a good plan to me," Buddha said.

"I'm for it," Mamudi said. "What's a litte more plastique among friends?"

"You realize this could cost us everything?" Bee asked.

The Marauders shifted about uneasily.

"But," Tom Bee added, "I suppose it wouldn't hurt to bring Jack back into the fold. After all . . . , he *is* a good soldier."

"One of the best," Mamudi seconded.

"Very dedicated," Buddha added.

"A real ass-kicker," Kinski chimed in.

"I even have a new glass eye for the occasion," Mamudi said, producing an orb that resembled a large cat's-eye marble. "Something wild, jungle-like."

"I'm sure that will rouse the troops," Bee muttered. "MacGregor? What do you think?"

MacGregor straightened his massive frame. "Well," he said, attempting wisdom, "we were planning one diversion anyway. I suppose it wouldn't hurt to plan a second. It'll get the FSE boys runnin' hither and yon and give us a better shot of getting the train out from under wraps and high-balling the hell out of here."

Bee smiled thinly. "Well then. It seems to be settled. To-night we depart for Aberdeen in two groups. But first we get Jack up and about to join us. Agreed?"

The men and Katt nodded as one. "Agreed."

"There's only one thing I don't like about it all," Bee said.

"What's that?" Kinski asked, repocketing his comb.

"Jack will be with the FSE for" —he glanced at his watch—"eight hours."

"So?" Kinski replied.

"Suppose by the time we hit the jail, he's no longer alive," Bee said.

The Marauders lapsed into silence. MacGregor stared down

at his shattered hand, rubbing it tenderly with his good one. "He'll be alive," he swore. "He *must* still be alive."

He looked up at the men, his face red, hardened. "And if, God forbid, he isn't . . . , we'll alter our plans a bit."

"Howso?" Bee asked.

"We'll take every lousy FSE bastard out in this town before we board the train."

Buddha Chan lowered his shades down to the tip of his nose, a Buddha wearing granny-glasses. "You know, MacGregor," he said with a grin, "for a foreigner, you have very American ideas."

ELEVEN

Crazy Jack Keenan tightened his stomach as the two blond giants began punching his mid-section again. He was held suspended in the old jail cell by two thick ropes.

The FSE men pummeled him for the upteenth time.

He feld his muscles contract and the air shoot up from within his lungs. Another couple of rounds and his kidneys would be worthless.

"Aren't you two getting bored?" he hissed.

The two giants retreated and glanced at each other. In truth, they were. But they had orders. Break the man. The problem was, the red-haired giant didn't seem to be breakable.

Abruptly they left the cell.

Crazy Jack stood there, immobile. His arms, spread-eagled in the air crucifixion-style, ached. His stomach was beyond pain at this point. His knees sagged, but he couldn't allow them to head for the floor. He'd rip his arms out of their sockets.

He laughed at himself. The things he got himself into. Jesusfuck.

A wiry fellow danced into the room. He reminded Crazy Jack of Jimmy Cagney. The elfin man didn't introduce himself, but by his manner of speech Jack knew he was Irish.

"How are we doing, Yank?"

"Fucking fine, Mick," Jack grinned back.

The wide smile on the elfin man's lips faded. "Haven't told us much, have you?"

"Don't have much to say," Jack replied.

"Oh, but you *do*," the elf said, walking up to Jack's massive, battered form. "You just haven't had the, ummmm, proper *encouragement*. For the record, Yank, we know all about your friends. All about the resistance. All about your plans."

Jack heaved a sigh. "I have no friends. I have no plans. The only resistance I applied today was against three Red bastards who tried to paw a female friend of mine. Pretty good resistance, too, I think."

"You're not telling me what I want to hear."

"How's this?" Jack began. "It's an old tale I know from my childhood."

The little man kicked Jack above the right knee. It was all Keenan could do not to collapse on it.

"Once upon a time," Jack began, "a chicken found a dime. He gave it to the rooster. The rooster said, 'It's mine.' "

Jack suddenly remembered his mother chanting that rhyme to him over and over in an effort to get him to sleep. He remembered himself, years later, chanting the same rhyme over and over to his own kids while, from the corner of the mobile-decorated bedroom, his wife smiled. He remembered the face of his mother. The faces of his children. The face of his wife. A sense of serenity swept through him.

"Once upon a time," he began to mumble again.

"This is crazy," the elf spat.

"I'm crazy," Jack said.

"Let's see if we can bring you to your senses."

Jack's vision swam as he felt himself being cut down.

He saw countless faces in front of him, mostly East European. His wrists were tied behind him. He felt his arms being pulled up high behind his back. His shoulder bones were ready to pop.

The elf's face loomed before him. "What's it all about, Yank? What are your plans?"

"Once upon a time," Jack began. His arms were lifted higher behind him.

His body was sagging forward. He was losing consciousness. He fought it off. Use the pain. Use the pain to stay alert. Remember mom, the kids, Deb.

"A chicken found a dime."

He was hoisted higher.

"He gave it to the rooster."

"I'm not fooling around, Yank!" the elf yelled.

"And the rooster said, 'Fuck you, you twisted little Mick bastard.' " Jack smiled.

Blackness.

When Jack awoke, he found his body tied to a chair, bound securely by rubber cords. His head began to roll. He noticed that the cords were slicing into his flesh. He didn't really feel it, but it was an interesting sight.

Damp.

He felt damp.

Sweat? No. Wet washcloths were being wrapped around the already too tight cords. Nice of them, he thought. What are they trying to do, make me catch cold?

It was then that he saw the elf's dancing legs. They were dancing next to a large battery. Was it a car battery? He couldn't see. He didn't care. When he heard the wires crackling nearby, smelled the faint aroma of ozone, his interest in the make of the battery faded.

"One more time, Yank," the elf demanded. "Why are you here?"

"Vacation." Jack grinned.

The elfin hands placed the wires on the damp cloth. Jack's body rocked back and forth in the chair.

He could feel the electricity slice through every fiber of his being.

"Once more?" the elf demanded.

"Remind me to . . . to change my travel agent," Jack gasped. "This is not a party town."

The wires made contact again.

Jack felt his head slam backward against the chair. He felt something stir up within him. Not anger. Not rage. Just pain, sheer pain. He opened his mouth to vent it. Even the elf backed off when the roar emerged from Jack's mouth.

It was loud, thundering, angry and vengeful.

When he was done, Jack allowed his mouth to remain open. Phlegm bubbled forth. His head tilted to the side. His body seemed wracked by fever. He felt every nerve ending in his body tingle. Think of mom, the kids, Deb.

He began to chuckle.

"What the hell is so funny?" the imp asked.

"Once upon a time," Crazy Jack began.

"Shut up!" the imp said, throwing down the wires and slapping Jack in the face.

Jack took the blow, his head slamming toward his left shoulder. "Sure," he muttered.

"You don't get it, do you?" The imp seethed. "It's all over for you. It's all over for your pals. Don't you get it?"

"I get it," Jack mumbled. "It's all over."

"We *know* everything you've planned. We *know* every move you make. *Your* source is *our* source. You idiots are dead men. How long will it take before you realize it?"

"I dunno," Jack whispered. "What time is it now?"

The imp instinctively glanced at his watch. He quickly put down his right arm. "You crazy, sad sonofabitch."

The imp marched across the room, James Cagney in a snit. He motioned to the half dozen FSE guards in the room. "Take this stuff out of here. Cut him loose and put him in another cell. A cell with no light."

The henchmen nodded.

Jack felt the rubber cords leave his body. He took a deep breath. He fought nausea. His body wasn't used to breathing deeply anymore. He felt his arms sag as the constraints were ripped away. His hands were numb. His shoulders ached. He couldn't feel where his legs should be.

Not a friendly bunch at all, he thought. But they were determined; he gave them that.

But the elf. The elf had told him something important. If only he could remember it.

He felt a half dozen tentacles wrap themselves around his body. He was being lifted. That was it. He was being carried somewhere. He tried to get his eyes to remain open. No dice. He blinked several thousand times.

The ceiling moved above him.

Latrine-green lights shone down on his weary, tear-stained eyes.

Mucus ran from his nose.

He had to remember what the elf had said.

The mission depended on it.

He was flying through air now. He saw a cot. His head slammed into the side of it. He felt the clammy, cold concrete floor beneath his naked feet. He heard a metal door slam behind him. He attempted to twist his body up onto the cot. He couldn't. He floundered on the floor, squirming, turning.

Bars loomed before him. Concrete walls. A solid metal door. Small window. Smaller bars.

He was stuck.

He might never see his comrades again.

He rolled his limp body against the concrete wall of the cell. He pressed his battered face up against the gray slab. It was cool. It robbed him of his fever.

He remembered the imp. He chiseled every feature of the little Irishman into his mind. Payback. He'd have payback. But the imp talked too much.

What was it he had said?

Why had it been important?

Jack lapsed into a deep, exhausted sleep. He remembered his mom, his kids, Deb. He recited one last prayer before he drifted off into an unconscious state, more of a faint than slumber. "Once upon a time, a chicken found a dime, he gave it to the rooster, the rooster said, 'It's mine.'"

Such was the stuff sanity was made of.

TWELVE

MacGregor, Freddie Mamudi, Kinski, Buddha Chan, Tom Bee and Katt paced the walls along the Argyle Battery of the Castle. They patted the ancient cannons still left from the 1730s, the Six Gun Battery, as they walked.

"There's not too much activity down there," MacGregor offered.

"Not to worry," Katt said, running a hand through her long brown hair, "we'll hear soon."

"Is the train ready?" Kinski asked, adjusting the wave on his coiffe in the moonlight.

"Fueled and raring to go," Katt replied. "We have four men who work at the depot."

"What about the troops?" Buddha asked, staring up at the stars from the mighty castle walls.

"Armed and ready to move out. We have cars, cycles, trucks and a few four-wheel drive vehicles ready."

"Any of them military issue?" Kinski asked.

"Afraid not," Katt replied.

"No armor?" Buddha asked.

"No," Katt said.

"We're in great shape," Tom Bee muttered. "Welcome to the Second Children's Crusade."

"Knock it off, Bee," Buddha said. "We'll do okay."

Tom nodded. "Sorry." He was edgy. He couldn't help it. He remembered the first time he was sent into combat. He was raw. Green. It was supposed to be a demilitarized zone. Half of the men were given bad ammo for their M-16s.

The only problem was that the VC had rifles with good ammo. Good aim, too.

Soon the DMZ flowed red with American blood.

Tom Bee had lived while most of the others had died, a look of shock and surprise etched on their faces as they spiraled toward the ground.

Ever since that day he made sure he was equipped to go into combat and that his fellow soldiers were up to snuff. But this mission? It was fugazi from the word go.

The Santa Claus figure of McClennen waddled up to the Castle's top wall. "We're ready, Katt."

Katt nodded. "All right, gentlemen, it's time we move out."

The Marauders nodded. MacGregor stood at the Castle wall, patting its ancient rock piling. "I'll be sorry to see this all go," he said. "It's part of our history."

"And we're part of your future," Buddha said, gently leading the Scot away from the wall. "Sometimes you have to let the past go. *We all do.*"

MacGregor nodded sadly and watched the Freedom Fighters line the walls with dynamite. "Make sure to wire the first level as well," he said. "We'll send the whole bloody thing tumbling down on their heads."

Katt smiled sadly as she led the Marauders and MacGregor down from the high walls to the base of the Castle. "Good luck," she said to MacGregor, Buddha and Kinski. "I hope Jack is all right."

"He'll be fine," Kinski said, "if his insides are half as strong as his outsides."

Tom Bee and Freddie Mamudi took their places behind the diminutive woman. "We'll see you at Aberdeen, my brothers," Bee said.

"I'll wink for you there," Mamudi said, patting his cat's-eye.

MacGregor smiled. "You take care of yourselves."

He walked up to Katt and gave her a massive bear hug. "Especially you, little girl."

"I'll be fine, Shatterhand," she said, returning the hug. "McClennen will go with you to the station. And, by the by, when you pick up Jack at the prison, well, we've arranged a little calling card for you."

Two of the Freedom Fighters brought out an old M-79, in great shape.

"A grenade launcher?" MacGregor said.

"Where the hell did you get that?" Kinski laughed. He was an old hand at using the weapon, but he hadn't seen one in years.

"The Irish-Americans used to be very generous to the IRA cause." Katt smiled. "They frequently used Scotland as a conduit. I thought it might come in handy someday."

"Come on, lads," McClennen told the Marauders. "Your friend and a train are awaiting us."

Kinski, Buddha and MacGregor nodded, walking over to the back of the truck.

McClennen got in behind the wheel and revved the engine. "Aberdeen and Freedom," the gnomelike man called as the truck pulled away.

"Aberdeen and Freedom," Katt called back, Tom Bee and Mamudi flanking her.

MacGregor sat between Buddha and Kinski, staring at the imposing structure of Edinburgh Castle as it faded into the distance. "The last time I'll see you," he whispered to the Castle. "You've stood long and proud to protect this city. May your sacrifice protect it longer."

"It will," Buddha said softly. "You have to believe that, Mac."

MacGregor nodded.

Crazy Jack Keenan felt the explosion before he heard it. He awoke from his stupor and, his head still spinning, clambered up on his bunk, chinning himself up to the small window positioned high upon the west wall of his cell.

Outside, the air seemed charged with fire.

He could hear the FSE goons inside the prison, running and yelling like madmen.

"The Castle!" someone screamed.

Jack chuckled to himself, lowering himself down onto the cot. The mission had begun. He heard one roar after another cut through the stillness of the night. Plaster fell from the cell's ceiling. "Nice demo job," he muttered.

He slowly walked to the cell door. He spied the Irish imp leaping through the halls, ordering the troops into combat-ready status. "To the rock! To the rock!" he cried. His voice emerged as a frightened squeak.

Jack settled down in his cot. It didn't matter what happened to him now. He had bought the time that Mac and the Marauders had needed. That was good enough for him.

He decided it was time to sleep and regenerate his energy. He stretched out on the cot and closed his eyes. He began drifting off into a deep sleep when he heard a familiar ka-thump.

He sat up in the bed, his face a living question mark. "Incoming?" he thought to himself.

Jack was thrown from his cot as the front of the jail was blown away. He heard screams from outside. Ka-thump.

He rolled under the cot. "Incoming," he stated flatly.

Smoke and the smell of burnt, charred flesh rolled into the cell.

Another roar.

Another chorus of surprised screams. Footsteps. All around him. Bullets started to zing by the metal door of his cell. Firefight. Small arms. Automatics. Semis. He heard screams. He heard curses in languages he had never encountered before. He curled up against the cell wall beneath his cot.

Ka-thump.

He closed his eyes as the entire cell was bathed in a tongue of fierce, white light. He heard the large metal door sail across the room and smash into the wall nearest him. The room was filled with dense, choking smoke. Still barefooted, Jack struggled to his feet. He gazed at the ruptured doorway. He seemed to be gazing into hell.

Flames licked the hallways outside. The walls dribbled blood and small wads of flesh. Illuminated by the flame, a titanic shadowshape appeared in the doorway. Satan? Death? Worse?

The figure stepped into the cell, flanked by a small, rotund figure and a lanky, wiry one.

"Come on, Jack," the first figure boomed. "It's time to go."

As the flames roared up behind them, MacGregor, Kinski and Buddha Chan padded into the room.

"Jesusfuckingchrist," Kinski exclaimed, catching sight of Jack's battered body in the flickering light provided by the inferno outside. "What did they do to you?"

Jack tried to smile. All he could muster was a wan smirk. "The usual."

"Come on," Buddha said, lifting Jack's titanic body on his short, squat shoulders and heading him toward the blown-out doorway. "We have to go."

"Did they hurt you, lad?" MacGregor said, seeing the deep cuts in Jack's back and torso.

"Naah," Jack said, "you know how it is. Dynamic tension. Isometrics. Builds muscle and character from within."

Jack promptly passed out.

Buddha Chan carried him out into the hallway. Kinski cradled his AK-47, and MacGregor carried a Remington 12 gauge in his hand. Most of the FSE troops lay dead or dying around them.

The trio, Jack strewn across Buddha's back, hobbled out of the wrecked prison. Above the town the remnants of Edinburgh Castle continued to erupt, the charges of dynamite going off at regular intervals.

Spriraling tongues of light and flame shot high into the air above the city with resounding roars, sending tons of boulder-sized slabs of rock and concrete tumbling down onto the advancing FSE troops.

Buddha tenderly laid Jack down in the back of the truck. McClennen, stroking his Santa Claus beard, gazed mournfully at the ever-erupting Castle.

"It was a fine place, that," he whispered.

"Yes," MacGregor said, sliding in the cabin beside him. "But we have to leave it now. We have a train to catch."

"That we do," McClennen said, shifting the truck into gear.

With all available FSE troops en route to the crimson-encased Castle, McClennen was able to point the truck directly toward Edinburgh railway station. In the back of the truck Buddha and Kinski stared at Jack's blood-caked, burn-marked body.

Jack revived for a moment. "Have we made it?"

"Just about," Buddha said.

"Good," Jack said.

"Anything broken beyond repair?" Kinski asked.

"Naah," Jack wheezed, his body suddenly wracked with a spasm of coughing. "But you know what the real bitch about all this is?"

"No," Kinski said, "tell me."

"My shoes," Jack said. "They cut off my fucking shoes."

Kinski smiled at Jack. Buddha nodded sagely. "We'll get you a new pair."

"Do you know how much that pair cost me?" Jack said, shaking his head from side to side. "Those heathen sonfa-bitch bastards."

THIRTEEN

Katt, Freddie Mamudi and Tom Bee huddled in the ammo-stacked Subaru 4-wheel-drive turbo, a good dozen years old. Katt was behind the wheel. Behind them Edinburgh Castle radiated heat and fire, spewing rock and violence into the air with a series of resounding thuds.

The car sped out of town unimpeded by FSE interference. Behind them some seventy other vehicles ground gears, beating a hasty escape.

"We're on our way," Katt breathed.

Mamudi nodded silently, sitting in the back seat with enough live ammo, weaponry and explosives to blow him sky-high if hit by a stray slug. He hoped Jack was all right. Tom Bee, in the passenger side of the front seat, stared at the trees whizzing by the car in the darkness.

"He'll be all right," he said softly.

"Huh?" Mamudi said, shaken from his private thoughts.

"Jack will be all right," Tom Bee replied.

"How can you tell?"

"I just *know*, so dismiss it from your mind. We have other things to consider right now."

"Yes," Mamudi nodded. rubbing his glass eye absent-mindedly. "Right."

Katt continued to pour it on. "No time to feel maudlin,

73

gentlemen. We have many stops to make on the way to Aberdeen.''

The car lurched along the old roadway, sending Mamudi tumbling into the boxes of ammunition. "You *have* driven this way before, haven't you, Miss Shea?"

"Many times," Katt laughed, catching the tension in Mamudi's voice. "I used to drive an egg truck. Never lost a yolk."

"I wasn't worried," Mamudi said, staring at the back of her beautiful head. "So," he said, "you are married?"

"No."

"You are engaged?"

"No."

"Attached?"

"No."

"Available?"

"Not for the likes of you," Katt laughed. "So you can stop making eyes at me in the rearview mirror. Oh, excuse me," she said with a grin, "*eye* at me."

Freddie laughed. He liked this woman. He really did. He would be proud to bed her. Proud to have her be the mother of a child. Sorry to leave her. Happy to return.

Katt caught his expression in the mirror. "Don't even think of it, Popeye."

Freddie grinned. "No one has called me that in a long time," he said. "Since before the war."

"It fits."

"Indeed." Mamudi nodded. "I was a sailor, of sorts."

"Then hold onto your spinach; we have a lot of miles to cover tonight."

"Have you ever thought of marriage?" Freddie pressed.

"Have you ever thought of levitation?" Katt replied.

"Many times," Freddie grinned, running a finger along his scar. "Haven't you?"

"Never." Katt smiled.

She pressed her foot to the gas. Mamudi snuggled deep into the recesses of the rear seat. He glanced at the terrain around him.

He caught some movement in the underbrush.

"Miss Shea?"

"Yes, Freddie?"

"Do you believe in little people?"

"I never thought about it."

Mamudi reached for his M-16. "What do you call the little people in Scotland?"

"We don't have any," Katt replied. "In Ireland they're known as leprechauns."

Mamudi rolled down his window. "I just saw one."

"What?"

"A very small man on an off-road bike. Seemed Irish to me."

"What did he look like?" Katt asked.

"Like someone familiar. An actor," Mamudi replied.

In the front seat Tom loaded an arrow into his mini-crossbow, his body tense.

"Color of hair."

"Yellow."

"Shit," Katt said, pouring on the gas. "It's O'Malley."

"The FSE man?" Bee asked.

"The biggest one around," Katt muttered. "We have to get the hell out of here, fast. If you see him again, kill the bastard."

Freddie Mamudi flinched as he heard the distinct crack-crack-crack.

He cradled his weapon as the glass behind him shattered. The car swerved violently.

He felt as if he was underwater. He slowly clawed his way up from the back seat of the car in time to hear Tom Bee thunder, "No!!"

Mamudi watched in horror as the back of Katt Shea's head slowly began to dissolve. Her head lurched forward, her face bursting forth against the interior windshield. He tried to reach up toward her, but he knew it was too late.

The second shot smashed into the nape of her neck, causing her head to slip round and round in a full circle. Her throat burst forward, nearly decapitating her.

Mamudi cried out in anguish as the once-beautiful woman was reduced to a driving dummy, its fragmented skull barely clinging to its spine. The blood-and-hair-topped skull bobbed and weaved before him as the car veered this way and that.

Bee reached over and yanked the wheel hard to the right.

He slammed his foot down across the body and hit the brake. The car lurched to a halt.

Mamudi pushed open the back door and rolled onto the ground. He heard the off-road bike roar in the distance, farther and farther away. He slowly got to his feet.

The caravan behind him slowed.

He walked over to the driver's side of the car and gently eased the door open. Katt's nearly headless body tumbled out.

Mamudi bent over, cradling the smashed, ghoulish form in his arms. "I would have been proud to have you as a wife," he whispered, the blood and brain matter dribbling onto his lap.

A long tear crept down his thin cheek.

It dripped off his chin and landed on Katt's right breast.

"Mamudi," a towering Tom Bee announced from above him.

"Yes?"

"We have to keep moving."

"But, Miss Shea . . ."

"Miss Shea is no longer part of our mission. She has gone to another world. Drag her to the side of the road. Let her spirit be free of all *this*."

Mamudi nodded and dragged the buxom, beheaded body to the shrubbery. He placed her tenderly beneath a wild rosebush and murmured a brief prayer. He walked back to the vehicle. All the Freedom Fighters in the trucks and cars behind them were staring at the two men.

Waiting for a word. A sign. A signal.

"Do not mourn," Tom said. "She will become part of the earth. Her energy will mingle with that of the living things around her. New flowers will grow. They will keep her beauty alive."

Mamudi glanced at the caravan. The men were confused, impatient, frightened.

"What do we do?" Mamudi said.

"You ride shotgun," Bee said, sliding over into the blood-soaked driver's seat. "I'll navigate."

Mamudi trotted around to the passenger's side and climbed in as Bee shifted the car into gear. The car glided forward, leaving the remains of Katt Shea far behind, ever entwined with roses.

"Where are we going?" Freddie asked.

Bee clenched his teeth. "Forward," he said. "We sure as hell can't go back."

Freddie nodded.

"How will we find the other troops?" Mamudi asked.

"Let's hope they find *us*—before the FSE does," Tom said flatly, guiding the car on the twisting, turning road to no-where.

FOURTEEN

Buddha Chan slung Crazy Jack over his short, squat shoulders and ran, along with MacGregor, Kinski and McClennen toward the Royal Scotsman, leaving the truck behind. The city of Edinburgh, behind them, was a continuous source of thundering, flaming explosions.

Sirens howled through the night.

Gunfire could be heard echoing down distant streets.

All hell had, literally, broken loose.

A pock-marked, gaunt man with a Brillo pad of black hair perched high on his eagle's head named Pheerson ushered them toward one of the trains cars. "Come on. Come on."

Kinski hesitated before boarding the train. The vehicle looked like something from a classic Lionel train set, sort of a combination of the Little Engine That Could and the *Orient Express*. Illuminated by the bright orange plumes spewed out by the Castle behind the men, the train looked like a gift from the gods of Olympus.

"It's a beauty, isn't it?" McClennen said.

"It is," Kinski nodded. "And it's old. Are you sure it's going to make the climb?"

McClennen nodded. "That I am. Most of its cars have been around since 1863 when the Caledonian Railway and the London & North Western Railway companies pooled their efforts. The engine is a type 37 diesel locomotive. That skeletal fellow over there, Pheerson, was a top-notch engineer before the war. He'll get us through anything. It's not that long a journey. We'll be crossing the Lowlands to Glasgow, then we'll skirt the River Clyde and then switch onto the West Highland Line for the ascent alongside Loch Long into the Highlands. We'll be fine.''

Kinski grunted, looking at the ornate old cars.

"Come on inside," McClennen said.

Kinski scrambled onto the train as Pheerson sent the engine into motion. Before McClennen could hop on board, an FSE guard jumped out of the darkness, his rifle upraised. "Halt."

The small, Santa Clause-like Scot hugged the platform as a short burst of white hot lead seared the air above his head, slamming into the side of one of the metal sleeping cars. "Awww, Christ," he hissed, "doesn't anything come easy?"

Kinski ducked into the car as the slugs sliced by his knees. "I'm getting a little sick of this shit," he muttered to himself, his knees quaking involuntarily.

Kinski swung around and opened up on the guard with his AK-47. The FSE man's bullet-riddled body danced the dance of death before collapsing onto the station floor.

"How tall do you think he was?" Kinski yelled at McClennen as he pulled the rotund man aboard.

"I dunno," McClennen gasped. "About six-four or so."

"Good enough," Kinski said, diving off the train and running across the platform.

"What are you doing, man? Are you daft?" McClennen yelled. "We're pulling away, lad!"

"No, I'm not quite daft yet," Kinski yelled, running over to the guard, yanking off his boots. "Jack needs shoes."

Kinski caught a movement out of the corner of his eye. Three more FSE guards were running up to the train, rifles trained. "What's going on here? Explain yourself!"

"Don't have time," Kinski said, letting loose with five short bursts.

The first guard pitched forward, clutching his throat. The second one squeezed off a few rounds. The concrete near Kinski's left foot shattered and sent off plumes of dust into the air.

"Give me a break," Kinski wheezed, pulling the trigger toward him and illuminating the dimly lit station with a white-hot muzzle flash.

The remaining two FSE men flew backward into a long-abandoned luggage cart.

"Come on, boy!" he heard McClennen yell.

Kinski grabbed the boots and dove toward the train as it pulled out of the station and into the endless night before it. He leaped onto the train at the last possible minute, McClennen's pudgy hands yanking him inside.

"Are you all right?"

Kinski nodded. He put both his weapon and the boots in one hand and produced a pocket comb. "Damned near ruined my hair, though," he said, sliding the small plastic comb through his large, blond, front wave.

"Never slip up on your personal hygiene," he said to the roly-poly man at his side. "That's one of the first things you lose in combat. Once you lose that, you lose all sense of personal pride and you're as miserable as the poor guy next to you."

McClennen chuckled. "A rule to live by."

Inside the train Kinski was stunned by the opulence of the cars. "You like it, eh?" McClennen smiled.

"I've never seen anything like it."

"Few people have. The observation car goes back to 1892. The salon car, 1912. The dining car goes back to 1891. During the First World War it was part of a mobile headquarters for Earl Haig in France. It was retired and became the dining room of a fine house before it was restored to use on the *Scotsman*."

McClennen led Kinski through the train. "In its day, people said it was more la-de-dah than the famed *Orient Express*, don't you know?"

"I'd believe that." Kinski nodded, feeling somehow inferior to his surroundings; a mere grunt with a rifle and a pair of muddied boots in his soiled hands.

The train began to pick up speed. The flaming Edinburgh Castle was only a dot in the far distance as the train sliced through the dense countryside.

"Where's Jack?" Kinski asked.

"They brought him to the salon car," McClennen said. "This way."

The two shambled through the quivering train, from car to car, until they entered the salon car, sort of a reading room/ lounge on wheels. Jack sprawled out on a couch. In the light afforded by the train Kinski could see just how bad Jack's wounds were.

He felt himself emit a hiss. He fought back the words. Jack looked like a breathing piece of raw meat.

Buddha Chan, his glasses off, washed the wounds with a damp cloth. "They used pretty standard tactics," Buddha said. "Simple but pretty effective . . . on most men."

Jack smiled, fighting off exhaustion. "But not on me."

"No, Jack, not on you," Buddha said.

"Here," Kinski said, tossing the boots in Jack's direction. "You can see if these fit."

"Where'd you find them?"

"They had a sale at the train station."

"If they're not Buster Brown, I ain't gonna wear them," Jack grinned from beneath split lips.

A dozen or so Freedom Fighters sat in the car in silence, their M-16s ready to rock. They were nervous.

Kinski glanced out the window. The men had good cause to be apprehensive. As the train roared toward the Highlands, the landscape changed. The train was suddenly surrounded by flatlands that mutated into forests and small lakes, then back into flatlands. The earth around them was barren and unpopulated. Nothing but fields, trees and rocks.

Any spot would be the perfect spot for an ambush.

Anyone with half a brain could pick them off easily.

"What's in back?" Kinski asked McClennen.

"The observation car."

Kinski hoisted his AK-47 and went aft in the train. The small car was bullet-tipped in shape, looking like the first car of the Disneyland monorail. Cushioned seats and a small table inhabited the tiny chamber. Kinski aimed the AK-47 carefully and fired a short burst through one of the domed windows, sending it flying backward onto the receding track.

"I'll watch our ass," he said to McClennen. "Put two of your men up in the engine."

"Good thought, Yank." McClennen nodded.

"Do you know anything about trains?" Kinski asked.

"If it's a mechanical thing, I can run it," McClennen said, picking a sliver of glass from his white beard.

"Then grab a weapon and get up there, too," Kinski said. "If anything happens to Pheerson, you're going to have to highball the hell out of this bucket of bolts. I have a feeling this will be a more eventful trip than we bargained for."

McClennen laughed. "Aye, sir."

He disappeared through the portal, leaving Kinski sitting alone in the mangled observation car. The place was filled with dust. He reached up and shut off the light. No sense in being a bigger target than he had to be.

A cold damp wind whipped through the shattered window. Kinski inhaled. He smelled the damp earth. The budding trees. The blooming flowers.

He smelled death.

In the salon car Jack slowly regained his strength. "Easy there, Keenan," Buddha said.

"Of, fuggit," Jack said, sitting up. "You're no Florence Nightingale. Let me try on these shoes."

He slipped on the dead FSE man's boots. They were a little big, but they'd suffice. "Did the others make it out?"

"We can only hope," MacGregor replied.

"They made it," Jack said, ignoring the shards of pain shooting through his body. "I have a feeling about matching Bee with Mamudi. They're both spiritual, in their own way. They'll do fine."

"You're not getting religious on us, are you?" MacGregor asked.

"Nope. It's the New Age Physicist coming out," Jack said. He stopped suddenly, surprised.

"What is it?" Buddha asked, replacing his shades firmly over his eyes.

"The dwarf."

"Huh?"

"The little Irish guy."

"Jeeezus," MacGregor said, "that was the man who did this to you?"

"Uh-huh. Little sonofabitch. Danced around the room like an old musical flick."

"Ian O'Malley. Top FSE dog in this territory."

"I don't care if it was Spuds McKenzie," Jack said, scratching his bruised forehead. "He said something to me during the interrogation. Something important. Something I just can't quite remember. I was half out of it. But I remember thinking, 'He's just told me more than I could ever tell him.'"

Jack ran his hand over his forehead, trying to massage his brain back to life. "The little bastard was so sure of himself. He taunted me. Laughed at what we were trying to do. He thought he knew everything, but I could tell he was hurting for information. He was missing vital parts of his plan. Yet he knew about the set-up. He tipped his hand. I just can't remember how."

"I don't understand," MacGregor replied.

"Douse the lights," Jack said abruptly.

The men in the car did just that.

"All you men," Jack said to the Freedom Fighters, "spread out in the cars. Take positions on each side and be ready for anything."

All the men turned toward MacGregor. MacGregor nodded assent.

"What is it, Jack?" MacGregor asked.

"We've been set up, Mac," Jack said, getting to his feet. "I just remembered what the little fucker told me."

"And what was that?"

"Your source is our source," Jack breathed.

"What the hell does that mean?" Buddha asked.

"*That's* why we've had the FSE chewing our butts since we got here. *That's* why every move we make, the FSE boys know it in advance. The same fellow who's giving us information from occupied London is tipping off the FSE. He's getting bucks from both sides."

"Montrose?" MacGregor gasped.

"Yeah." Jack nodded. "Whoever the hell he is in real life."

MacGregor slumped into a large, plush chair, "Oh, Jesus God," he moaned.

"Don't worry about it," Jack said. "We'll outmaneuver him. I've been in worse situations."

"You don't understand," MacGregor moaned. "Montrose is joining us at Aberdeen."

"What?" the Buddha exclaimed.

"*He's* the one who's been tipping us off to the movements of the FSE troops. He's going to link up with the caravan. Lead them into Aberdeen."

"Christ," Jack muttered. "Tom Bee? Mamudi?"

"They'll be driving right into Montrose's open arms," Buddha exclaimed.

Jack scanned the countryside whizzing by the train. "Well, they're big boys, They'll take care of themselves. I'm sure of it."

"And if they don't?" MacGregor asked.

"Then we and your Clansmen will have quite a job cut out for us at Aberdeen. That sonofabitch Montrose . . . taking payoffs from both sides. He must be one rich weasel right about now."

"Aye." MacGregor nodded.

"And do you know what?" Jack asked.

"What?"

"When we get to Aberdeen, he's going to be one *dead* little weasel."

MacGregor smiled grimly. "True enough, Jack, my boy. But *I'm* going to be the one to send him to the afterlife."

Jack shrugged, still watching the countryside for any signs of life. "Fuggit. It's your country."

The train roared through the fog-shrouded night.

The longest night in the world.

FIFTEEN

Mamudi and Bee kept their vehicle well ahead of the caravan. If there was any trouble, they'd take it before the rest. Using a torn and dog-eared roadmap, they navigated the foggy road.

The car bumped along. More than once, Mamudi glanced nervously in the back seat where the ammo, a few weapons, explosives and a half-dozen grenades swayed gently.

Mamudi glanced to the right and left of the small vehicle as it sped along. Bee kept his eyes on the stretch of winding concrete before him.

"Anything?" Bee asked.

"Not so far."

"We'll hit it soon," Bee said.

"Do you *feel* it?"

"No," Bee answered, "but it makes sense, doesn't it? This O'Malley fellow is somehow plugged into our every move. He knew everything we . . . "

Ka-thump.

"Incoming," Mamudi gasped.

"Don't I know it."

An M-79 grenade burst before them, temporarily obliterating the road. Bee yanked the wheel to the left. Hard. "Grab the C-4 and the blasting caps and let's ditch'' he yelled as another grenade lashed out at the trees next to the car.

"But the car!!!" Mamudi yelled.

"We can always get another goddamned car," Bee rumbled.

The car pin-wheeled off the road. The two men tumbled from the car, each man clutching his weapons, Bee grabbing a lone M-60 from the back seat and enough ammo to keep them going for a few minutes. Mamudi snatched the C-4 and a few grenades.

The two men hunched down by the side of the road. "Fucking number ten." Mamudi said.

"You've got that right," Bee said, standing and pumping the machinegun into the night for all it was worth. "Wave the other cars forward."

Mamudi stood and frantically motioned the caravan onward, full-tilt speed. "Get the hell out of here!" he yelled, with Bee still firing madly at any sign of movement.

Mamudi saw the puzzled faces of the Scots in the cars and trucks. They were eager to make a stand. Eager to fight. "We'll catch up with you. Don't worry!" he bellowed.

Bee continued firing. He glanced at Mamudi, who was reaching for a grenade. "Save it." he said flatly.

Mamudi replaced the grenade on the ground. "For what?"

"We'll need it later."

The caravan barreled onward, the macadam around it shattering under the impact of each new assault. Some of the Scots returned the fire, trying their best to keep the FSE sappers at bay.

Soon all the vehicles had passed. The ka-thump sound continued. The road continued to be destroyed. Only the two Marauders remained.

"It's been really nice knowing you, Tom," Mamudi said, diving into a small ditch on the side of the road as a spray of concrete and dirt pounded into his back.

Bee stopped firing. He was out of ammo.

"We're not dead yet," he whispered.

"A technical point," Mamudi said. "And I thought the tiger eye would do it."

"It may yet," Bee said, pointing to a barn two hundred meters away.

"Remember the Alamo?" Bee smiled.

"The John Wayne flick?" Mamudi asked.

The Native American heaved a sigh.

"It was before your time," Bee answered, swinging his massive frame toward the old stone structure. "Shag it."

The two men ran for the stone barn, the earth rupturing all around them.

They entered the thirty-by-thirty structure, slamming the wooden door behind them.

"Fine," Mamudi said. "Now we can die in an avalanche of rocks instead of just getting blown up real good."

Bee looked at the younger man. "You were a SEAL, right?"

"Right."

"Look around you and use your head."

Mamudi squinted his good eye and took stock of what was in the barn. Nails. Discarded bottles Diesel fuel. Rags. Old metal tubing. Bailing wire. Fishing twine. Electrical tape. Shovels. Pitchforks.

"An arsenal." He beamed.

"You start working on the inside," Bee said. "I'll start doing up the outside."

Bee grabbed a wad of fishing twine and three grenades. A shovel. A pitchfork. "Right about now, the FSE troops are trying to figure out what to do. Go after the caravan or blow our brains out. My guess is that we'll be the target. We're the new, big names in town. Parading our bodies in front of the citizens will have a profound effect."

"Rah, rah, rah," Mamudi said, taking the nails from their boxes.

Bee made for the door. "We have fifteen minutes, tops, so work quickly. I'll be back as soon as I can."

"Have a care out there," Mamudi said.

"Don't sweat it, brother," Bee said, disappearing into the darkness. "We'll teach those boys a lesson they'll never forget. Never underestimate heart, soul and a nimble brain."

In the darkness Tom Bee worked silently and efficiently. Using shards of shattered tree limbs as stakes, he lined the front of the barn with an almost invisible tripwire some six inches above the ground, hooking the pins of the three grenades onto the taut string of death every twenty yards. He could have used a dozen grenades more, but three would have to do.

Retreating toward the barn, he spotted a grenade crater, tit high, in the ground.

Breaking the pitchfork in two, he jabbed the pointed half into the bottom of the crater and covered the hole with stray shrubbery, making sure the top of the crater looked flat and natural. It wasn't as good as punji stakes, but it would have to suffice.

Inside the barn Mamudi worked hard preparing for the inevitable assault.

Carefully cutting the C-4 plastique explosive into blocks, he took great caution in pressing a round stick into the center of each charge to make room for the blasting cap. He reached for the electrical tape, cutting off a dozen foot-long strips. He carefully placed the nails, one by one, onto the tape, making sure that the nails were pressed tightly together. That done, he wrapped the nails firmly around the explosive, completely covering the four sides of the block. Not having regular fuses, he found a length of rope and cut off twelve rope fuses, attaching the blasting caps onto the rope shards using a pair of pliers. Sweat forming on his scarred brow, he carefully placed the blasting caps in the holes of the plastique blocks. He taped the rope cords securely in place. Nothing would shake them loose.

When he was done, Mamudi grinned.

He had just created twelve very effective fragmentation grenades from scratch.

He then gathered every available bottle in the barn and filled them with diesel fuel. Dipping small rags into the remainder of the fuel, he jammed them into the bottles. Nothing like an old-fashioned Molotov cocktail to shake people up. Twenty of them. That would give the FSE something to think about.

Bee entered the barn. "How is it going?"

Mamudi sat back, "I think I just earned an 'A' in science."

Bee grinned. "Fine. Let's get this stuff out of here and move behind the barn."

"I thought we were going to take them on here," Mamudi said.

"That's exactly what the FSE thinks as well," Bee replied, gathering up the frag grenades. "Dip the fuses in the fuel, will you?"

Mamudi nodded and did so.

"They'll open up on the barn full-tilt," Bee said. "It's better that we be a ways behind it. When they think they've done us in and move in to bag our bodies, we'll open up."

Mamudi smiled. "I like the way you think."

Bee started carrying the explosives out of the barn. "It bothers the hell out of me."

The two men ran to a small hill at the back of the barn and waited, their small arsenal at their sides.

The wait wouldn't be long.

SIXTEEN

Ian O'Malley paced up and down in the damp darkness. Behind him three dozen FSE troops, barely able to understand English, loomed like gargoyles.

"We have to make an example of them," he told one FSE lieutenant.

The man nodded dumbly.

"You've royally fucked up so far," O'Malley spat. "I don't think Chairman Maximov will be too happy."

At the sound of the word "Maximov," the blond hulk of a lieutenant snapped to. O'Mally smiled. "So here's your chance to redeem yourself. There's two of them. Thirty of you. Do you think you can handle them for the Chairman?"

The man nodded, his tongue caught in his mouth like an idiot's.

"Fine," O'Malley said. "Get them."

The lieutenant, whose name was Gatzen, offered a stiff salute.

"Awww," O'Malley said with a flick of the wrist, "get away from me now. I'll get back to Edinburgh and let London know what a fuckup you've made of things. You know where to find me when things are done."

Gatzen grinned and nodded. He motioned his troops forward. Armed with AK-47s and M-16s, the FSE men slogged toward the barn. Even without ammunition for their M-79s, they figured their numbers and firepower could eliminate the two intruders in the old stone barn.

They were mistaken.

Gatzen ordered six men forward and pointed toward the barn.

Point-men, Dead meat.

The East Europeans nodded and marched forward, their weapons trained. They were practically drooling at the idea of slaughtering the two Americans. They'd make an example of them.

Gatzen chuckled to himself.

This would be easy.

Very, very easy.

He was still chuckling when he saw the first man trip, falling over with a cry.

What the—?

The remaining five men rushed toward their fallen comrade, not knowing what had happened to the bulky boy. Gatzen hissed, sucking breath in between his clenched teeth as the night exploded before him.

The five men and their leader suddenly flew high into the air, their bodies slowly coming apart at the seams as the trip wire and the grenades proved their effectiveness.

The FSE troops gasped in unison as the bloody body parts slowly wafted to the ground, surrounded by smoke, fire, flesh and pieces of shit.

Gatzen grew angry.

The Americans were not playing fair.

If it was carnage they wanted, it was carnage he'd give them—with pleasure. He motioned the men forward. Guns blazing before them, the FSE troops charged the barn. Gatzen, in the lead, yelled in Czech for his men to hasten their pace. He was still yelling when he stepped on a small mound of fallen leaves.

He was still yelling when he tumbled into the pit and his neck met the prongs of a pitchfork. The metal fingers sliced through his jugular and cut off all thought from his brain. His body twitched on the farm tool for thirty seconds or more. Then it collapsed with a mighty sigh. The lieutenant moved no more.

The FSE troops, not noticing their leader's demise, continued the charge, weapons firing screaming slugs into the side of the stone structure, ripping up shards of wood from the massive, barred doors. Concentrating on the wooden portal, they reduced the doors to slivers. They barreled through the entranceway, guns still slicing up everything in sight.

Inside, they found . . .

Nothing.

The FSE grunts backed out of the ancient barn, not knowing where to turn. Their leader had disappeared. They trained their guns on the surrounding trees. On the hills. At the rocks. At anything.

It was at that point that one of the infantrymen exploded into flame. He staggered around his stunned fellow soldiers, screaming both communist rules and regulations as well as a hasty Hail Mary in Czech.

The troops stood there for one long second, not knowing where to run or where to charge.

A second man erupted.

A third.

A sergeant in the FSE outfit, Kozlowski, tried to rally his men. He motioned for a retreat. Mid-motion, he too felt the all-encompassing heat of a hand-thrown fireball. Dropping his rifle, he tried to beat off the advancing tongues of flame that seemed to be erupting from every pore in his body. When the flames reached his eyes and he felt both his sight and all signs of feeling melt, he opened his mouth to screech into the night sky. He couldn't, however, because a fist of flame slammed itself deep into his lungs. He staggered and simmered, finally collapsing into a heap before the startled eyes of a private, Malawka.

Malawka stood frozen in the middle of the inferno.

One by one, men all around him were exploding.

He didn't understand. This was not the kind of fight O'Malley had described.

The flaming men, flailing and screaming all around him, eventually collapsed onto the ground. Smoldering heaps. Nothing more. They reminded him of burning leaves back in his homeland. Fall. Many colors. He had the good sense to yell to the remaining men. "Retreat!" he bellowed.

At that point his body was sliced by a hundred small projectiles that had landed at his feet in a small brick. The nails twisted and turned through his body, making him feel as if he'd been crucified and then some. He tried to beat the nails away as if they had been nothing more than a swarm of invading bees.

The tactic didn't work.

He saw five fingers crumple as the metal fragments sliced through both flesh and bone.

Something entered his eye.

He felt his brain explode as the projectile bored upward. He tried to laugh. He tried to cry. Nothing worked. His bowels gave way.

Something sliced his throat.

He fell onto the damp earth of a country he knew nothing about, shitting, pissing and bleeding his life away.

The FSE men around Malawka panicked.

The Americans were devils.

They had *God* on their side.

The FSE men tried to make it back to their trucks. Make it back to their headquarters in Edinburgh. O'Malley would know what to do. He was in charge. He'd know how to counter-attack.

As the men ran toward their trucks, they felt the hot, tiny pincers of the flying nails invade their bodies. Arteries exploded. Livers burst. Intestines were slashed into tiny pieces.

The men continued to run, blinded by the flash of the charges and the pain of the frag grenades.

They reached for their guns, only to find that their arms wouldn't work. They stared at their limbs, now spouting blood like a fountain in the middle of the last plaza they had seen.

Eyes refused to work.

Ears were too deaf to hear.

Throats couldn't swallow the saliva, because they were inundated with fresh and unexpected blood.

A lone man survived the assault. He staggered toward the three four-by-fours left idling on the hillside. He'd make a report. He'd wreak revenge. O'Malley would back him. He was loyal to the Chairman. It hadn't been his fault.

The air behind his head whistled.

He didn't dare turn.

He reached for his rifle.

Before his hand could make contact with the stock, a small sliver of steel invaded his skull. The arrow smashed through the back of his head and emerged from his left eye. The man fell to the ground in a heap; his last thought was "What is that whistling noise?"

Then all was quiet.

The FSE troops lay dead and dying, strewn on the ground before the ancient stone barn. Smoke was everywhere. The stench of blood wafted up into the night air with it. From behind the barn Tom Bee and Freddie Mamudi emerged.

"What do you think?" Mamudi whispered.

"I think you're a damned good SEAL," Bee replied, walking forward through the smoke and debris.

"I mean about the FSE troops," Mamudi added.

"There isn't one left," Bee said, marching forward toward the truck.

"Where are you going?"

"I have an arrow to retrieve."

Mamudi danced over the dead and writhing bodies of the FSE goons.

"Hey, Tom? We're stranded out here."

"No we're not," Bee said, bending over a skewered body and yanking the small arrow out of its skull.

"All we have to do is take one of these trucks·and catch up with the caravan," the Native American said in a flat, dull tone. "No problem."

"But what about the little guy? O'Malley?"

"He has enough problems already," Bee smiled. "He's out in the cold. He fucked up. At least twice. That goes to a man's head. Makes his decisions a little less *rational*."

"Do you think he'll flip out?"

"Not for now. He won't know about this for at least two hours. That's two hours of driving time, Freddie."

Tom Bee walked up to one of the four-by-fours and slid behind the front wheel.

"Come on," he said. "We're moving out."

"Are you sure you know where we're going?" Freddie asked, scrambling into the passenger's side of the truck.

"No," Bee shrugged. "But if we keep on going forward, we can't be wrong."

Mamudi chuckled, slamming the door of the truck behind him. "I like the way you think, Mr. Bee."

"I like your company, Mr. Mamudi," Bee nodded, grinding gears and sending the truck forward on an endless road to freedom.

The truck tore out on the misty road. Freddie bounced around as the truck navigated its way past the potholes.

"Tom?" Mamudi asked.

"Yeah?"

"Why are you here?"

"Had no place else to go."

Mamudi nodded. "I'm not sure I get that."

"You're young," Bee said, "at least compared to me."

"You're not that old," Mamudi smiled.

"Just an eternity or so," Bee said, angling the wheel so it guided the truck past the craters in the blasted road.

"You see," Bee began, "when you were very, very young, there was a war. No, it wasn't a war. According to the Prez, it was nothing more than a police action. Hundreds of thousands of kids, and I mean *kids*, were sent to a country we didn't know squat about."

"Vietnam," Freddie injected.

"Yeah." Bee nodded. "I went back in '68. It was the strangest damned thing. Once you landed there, once you were in country, you just knew that you weren't going to win shit. Now, for someone like me, someone who grew up surrounded by nature, it was really a weird trip. The country was beautiful, really. I mean, if it hadn't been a war zone, you could spend the rest of your life there.

"I grew up surrounded by dry heat. Wet heat intrigued me. The rice paddies. The different hues of green. It was really something.

"But I learned fast that green could be a good cover for hell. There was no *sanity* there, Mamudi. After a week taking incoming rounds, sapper fire, you just clicked into the madness. You just tried to get through every minute, every hour. Organization? There wasn't squat.

"Half of the time, your lieutenant was greener than you were, shitting in his pants. He had no sense and less courage. Totally fucked. That put the burden on us guys, the grunts. You never knew where the hell you were or what you were there for. One day a hill would be A-priority. Take the sucker. Hunker in. By the time you got up there, it wasn't important anymore. You sat there like an idiot, the hill secured. Then you got your orders. Saddle up. Shag it.

"We were kids, Mamudi. We didn't know shit from shinola. Yet we were killers, too. After a while you didn't mind seeing the trophys some of the Vietnamese Army boys took. They'd come trotting into basecamp with a couple of heads on sticks. They'd post the heads after we moved out. It was sort of like flipping the bird to the VC.

"After a while we were doing strange shit, too. We'd gather up the VC bodies at the end of a day. Take mementos. Cut the VC's ears off. You proved how good you were by the number of ears you had on you. If you had a whole necklace of ears, you were one good killing machine. Guys were slogging around the jungle in a world they didn't know, carrying ears, noses, peckers.

"It was strange. It was numbing. The longer we stayed, the less we became. Everything was on auto, if you know what I mean. One minute, you'd be laughing with a buddy, taking a smoke, staring at the green around you and just sighing, 'Yeah, this is heaven.' The next minute, you'd be stuffing your buddy's intestines back in his gut and ducking for cover.

"Or you'd find a sapper and kill 'im. If it was a woman, you cut off her breast. Trophy time. The thing was, if you didn't do stuff like that, your officers thought that you were wrong in the head. It was one hellish time, Mamudi. No beginning. No end. Only *middle*.

"And the earth seemed to lash out at you. We'd hump all day, sometimes with rucksacks that weighed over a hundred pounds. You'd be lugging that stuff and trying to walk really daintily, like some kind of prima ballerina.

"You never knew what you'd step on. Solid ground gave way to a pit filled with punji sticks. Trip-wire frag grenades. Bouncing Bettys, though, they were the worst. You'd hit the sucker and it would bounce about three feet into the air. Waist level. If you tripped it, you were dead meat. Cut in two, just about. All the people around you could do was try to get down onto the jungle floor fast enough, so maybe they'd just get fragged a little bit. Half of the time we were out there, we were wired. You popped pills every day. You were just eyeballs and ears. Whatever speed was available, you took. You had to be alert. At night you'd toke up with the local weed—it was pretty heavily opiated—and try to get unconscious. It wasn't sleep, you understand. It was just a sense of limbo, of not being *aware*. I was a kid. A kid from a dinky town who didn't know *anything* about *anything*. I was too stupid to be scared.''

Bee stared at the road. ''My head really got done in over there. Stayed for three tours.''

''Why?''

''Seemed a lot safer than going back to the States.''

''How's that?''

''I dunno. It sounds stupid now, this many years after. I didn't feel that one place was any better or worse than any other. Wherever I puked my guts out was home. You see, when you're a Native American, an Indian, you're born fucked.''

Mamudi clearly didn't understand.

Bee continued, grappling with the wheel and gunning the gas. ''Imagine being the descendants of the forefathers of America.''

''Okay.'' Mamudi nodded.

''Then, imagine that your entire history had been wiped out. Erased.''

Mamudi blanched. ''I'm not sure I follow you.''

''Not to worry.'' Bee grinned. ''Not many *Americans* do. Let me put it to you bluntly. My people, no matter what the tribe, settled America. It was *our* land. We made it. We farmed it. We lived it. Nurtured it. And after the Europeans arrived, we were meant to feel as intruders. At every point in American history, we were driven out, systematically slaughtered.

''We were gathered as an alien nation and tossed onto barren tracts of land the government called reservations. We were told to live in peace and milk the land for whatever we could.''

''So?'' Mamudi asked innocently.

''So,'' Bee breathed, ''the land we were *forced* upon wasn't up to supporting a tribe, or a town, or *anything*. But we were *stuck*. Where could we go? We were a tribe. A family. The elders began to drink. Some of the younger braves began

taking potshots at any white man they could get within their
sights. It was hell. There was no hope. No dreams. Nothing
to look forward to. You either drank yourself into oblivion or
took thankless jobs. And those with jobs got in trouble with
the law. Every other weekend there were white lawmen coming onto the reservation dragging some poor buck off on a
drunk and disorderly charge. That's the world I grew up in.''

"Sounds like it sucked in a very existential way,'' Mamudi
whispered.

"It did. And moreso you never knew who was protecting
you or who was hunting you down. And in the middle of all
that shit, there was this insane belief that—somehow—Mother
Earth would rally to our defense. I kept that belief, returning
from Nam to spit and name-calling. I tried to behave like a
Native Warrior for as long as I possibly could. I would become one with the Land, like my Ancestors had.

"But by the time I got home, Mother Earth was poisoned.
It wasn't the same, ample womb I knew as a child. Crops
grew gnarled. Rain didn't come. Dust blew up like a slap in
the face for miles around.''

"And then?''

"I figured that a *new* America had to be formed. A country
who cared as much for its dispossessed as it did for its high
level bigwigs.''

"And what happened?''

"The last war happened.''

"And?''

"And suddenly minorities didn't matter as much. It was a
question of national survival. It was a matter of getting on as
a *country*. With all nationalities pulling together. So I came
out of retirement. I gave up the civilian life. I made it known
in the immediate area that if there was a just fight to be
fought, Thomas Bee would be there to fight it.''

"So that's how you joined the Marauders,'' Mamudi said.

"That's about it,'' Bee replied, still guiding the four-by-
four across the dusty macadam.

"How about you?'' Bee asked.

Mamudi felt the truck shake. "Just about the same,'' he
said, nodding as the fog began to invade the cabin of the
truck.

"I don't remember one hell of a lot about my childhood.

It was a brown, sandy place. We thanked Allah for every breath we took and every sunrise. Very close-knit. Families that were *families*. And then the Russians came in. My family fled before I was a teenager.

When I was a kid, I was playing outside in a place I suppose I shouldn't have been. A Russian sniper saw me and fired. I remember being suprised to feel my entire body sail through the air without any urging from me. The bullet slammed into my face.

"Took out an eye."

Mamudi felt the truck hit a bump. "I was young, so I got used to the scar. Got used to the glass eye. My father, though, got angry. He made every effort he could to get the hell out of there.

"Eventually he contacted relatives in New York, back when there was a New York.

"He pulled on some heavy strings. Got a load of black market money and arranged safe passage out of there. We moved to America. I became a naturalized citizen. As soon as I was able, I enlisted. Payback. That's the way I thought of it.

"They sent me all over the world. I worked a lot of 'police actions' in the Mideast. The CIA had the SEALs hopping around the Gulf. The funny thing was, the longer I stayed over there, the less idea I had of what I was doing or why. After a while patriotism didn't enter into it.

"It was a business. A job. Our job was terrorism. Keep the governments we didn't like guessing. Take out a leader and make the hit look like it was done by someone in the opposing party. Get them from within.

"It never amounted to much. It was just bullshit. Marking time.

"While I was away from home, the gangs began to invade the southeast Bronx, my family's neighborhood. My father was shotgunned in the middle of the afternoon one day. Just because he wouldn't hand over his wallet. My kid sister was beat up pretty badly. Almost crippled for life.

"My mother was going crazy. It all happened so fast. I had just gotten a furlough, some R and R time. I was going to head home to see what I could do for my family.

"Then the bombs dropped."

"There was no more place called home."

"How did you handle it?" Bee asked.

"I retreated. Turned to my religion. Meditated. That helped. That helped a lot. Sufism can be soothing. It emerged back in the late tenth century. Abu Said, Omar Khayyam. Jalad ad-Din Rumi. It's a very lyric train of thought, uniting one's soul with God. A little bit of Buddhism, a little bit of Christianity, a little bit of Neoplatonism. Parts of it urge asceticism, others quietism. All parts urge a quiet reunion with the Maker. All is One, no matter whether here or . . . *somewhere* else."

Bee nodded, gunning the truck onward.

Pretty soon he had the caravan back in sight. He smiled at Mamudi. "We work well together."

Mamudi leaned back in the passenger seat. "It was fate that brought us together. I truly believe that."

Bee smiled. "It's good to believe in something."

SEVENTEEN

The *Royal Scotsman* barreled along the track under the cover of darkness. On board, Crazy Jack, Kinski and Buddha Chan studied a wall map in the observation car. "They're going to hit us," Jack said. "It's just a matter of where and when."

MacGregor entered the car. "Trouble?"

"Coming up," Kinski said. "We're just trying to figure out the spot."

MacGregor stared at the map. "We've already gone past Glasgow. I thought we would have encountered some activity there. It's a big city."

"That probably worked out to our advantage," Buddha said. "All of Edinburgh knows that there's solid resistance leveled at the FSE, no use telling the entire population of Glasgow the same thing."

MacGregor nodded. "They wouldn't want a public uprising, would they?"

"Where's the toughest spot for us to negotiate with the train?" Jack asked.

"We'll be heading uphill to Kilpatrick, so we'll be slowing down a bit," MacGregor said. "After that, we pass Bowling."

"Isolated towns?" Kinski asked.

"Pretty much so."

"After that?" Kinski pressed.

"After Dumbarton we'll be crossing the River Leven. At Craigendoran we veer to the right and onto the West Highland Line proper. After that, we can bulldoze our way from Perth to Inverness in a matter of hours. The weather is with us. It'll be dank and cloudy for days on end. . . . I hope."

Crazy Jack sighed. "My guess would be they'll hit us before we take off for the Highlands."

He used his finger on the map. "Either here, by the river, or over *here* when it seems we're pretty high up."

"That we will be. The Erskine Road Bridge is a towering one."

"No chance of any of your supporters keeping the FSE at bay with a little H & I fire?" Kinski asked.

"Huh?" MacGregor blinked.

"Harassment and interdiction," Jack replied. "And that seems doubtful with a mole in the ranks."

"So we're stuck," Buddha said. "They can pretty much do whatever they want to us."

"Maybe." Crazy Jack smiled.

MacGregor looked up. "I don't like that look in your eye, Jack."

"Let's see what we have going for us. The FSE uses the track regularly for supplies, right?"

"Right."

"So they're not going to do anything that will destroy the track. They won't be blowing us off any bridge if it screws up their supplies. We're vulnerable until we reach the Highland Line but only up to a point. They could smash the Highland tracks, since they're not used anymore, but I don't think the FSE troops have the balls to go into unkown territory. There's no telling what the clansmen will do to them up there."

"You're right on all points." MacGregor said.

"But what are you leading up to?" Kinski asked.

"We have too much train," Jack said. "We could stand losing a few cars at the proper time."

He stared at the map. "Is there a switching yard nearby?"

"There is," MacGregor said. "About ten miles up the

track. It hasn't been used in years. It's not even a station anymore. British Rail nearly dismantled it years ago.''

"Fine." Jack grinned. "Tell Pheerson we'll be making a pit stop."

"And why is that?" MacGregor asked.

"We're going to change the configuration of our train a tad," Jack said grinning even more. "You see, the way I figure it, the FSE boys will try to slow us down somewhere along the pre-Highland Line.''

"A barricade?" Kinski asked.

"Could be an old-fashioned type. Could be vehicles. Whatever. They'll figure we'll try to plow through it, which in truth is what we're going to have to do. That will slow us down though. The engine will sustain damage, and when we're trying to regroup aboard the train, the FSE sappers can pick us off. Pretty neat. The track won't be damaged. They'll salvage most of the train. All will be right with the world.''

"But we're not going to do that," Buddha added, "are we?"

"We'll be forced to, but with a little difference." Jack said.

He turned to MacGregor. "Which cars are the heaviest? The sturdiest?''

"The sleeping cars," MacGregor said. "They're the newest additions. They're made of heavy metal and are the longest of any of them.''

"Fine, Jack replied. "When we hit the switching yard, have your men uncouple the sleepers and put them in *front* of the engine. The rest of the cars will remain where they are, but I want Pheerson or McClennen or whoever knows trains the best to make sure we can uncouple them whenever we want en route.''

"That's pretty dangerous," MacGregor said. "It'll have to be done manually.''

"What'll it take?" Jack asked.

"A crowbar, a wrench, maybe a sledge hammer," MacGregor said.

"Do we have any of that on board?" Jack asked.

"Maybe in the engine," MacGregor said.

"If we don't, we'll see what we can salvage from the switching yard," Jack said.

Kinski began laughing. "You're one crazy sonofabitch."

Jack grinned. MacGregor was still in the dark. "Don't you see?" Jack said. "We're going to be forced to play into the hands of the FSE, but it'll be okay. Those sleeping cars will make the best battering ram in history."

MacGregor emitted a loud, booming laugh. "There's a method to your madness then, eh, lad?"

"Always," Jack replied.

"We're still going to have problems," Buddha said, rubbing his chrome-dome absent-mindedly.

"How so?" Jack asked.

"Well, suppose we do manage to get by the FSE troops using the sleepers as a wedge. If the cars are derailed, we're screwed. The engine will follow them right off the track."

"That's a chance we'll have to take," Jack answered.

"And if they're not derailed, then we're stuck with extra weight in front of the engine just when we'll need extra power to get into the Highlands."

"Good point," Jack said. "Mac? Is there another switching yard between the next and when we hit the Highland Line?"

"There is, at the point where we make the shift."

"Then we'll just have to uncouple those cars and highball it," Jack answered.

"And what will the FSE troops be doing at that time?" Buddha asked.

"More than likely chasing after us like bats outta hell," Jack said.

"And what's to stop them from catching us?" Buddha queried, playing devil's advocate.

"Here's the deal, Buddha." Jack shrugged. "We can't play guerrilla games here. It's not going to cut it. We have to play straight and obvious. War. In capital letters. We can't get away with hit-and-run tactics.

"We don't have the time or the manpower to undermine the FSE. No terrorist tactics. We can't paralyze them with selective assassinations. Selective atrocities. We can't sabotage them in little ways and then slowly escalate. We're facing a timetable that's unreal.

"This is all very conventional. We're going to be reduced to putting our heads down and running full-tilt forward for half of this mission. It sucks, but that's the way things are. We don't have the advantage of surprise. We don't have the advantage of brilliant strategy.

"We came into this country beating a very loud drum. We didn't intend to, but that's the way things worked out. Now, if the FSE is on our ass, we just have to mow them down, take them out. We can't work from within their ranks. We can't even get off a recon team to fuck with their heads. What we have to do is clobber them. Right out in the open. Nail their asses to the trees."

Jack sighed. "I don't like it any more than you do. But those are the facts. When you don't have a lot of time to use your head, you have to use your fists."

"Pretty primitive," Buddha said. "I feel like a gladiator."

"You sure as hell don't look like one," Kinski cackled.

Buddha emitted a deep, rumbling chuckle. "I always had a thing for *Spartacus*."

"Not me." Kinski grinned. "I was kind of keen on *Ben-Hur*." He produced his comb and ran it through his hair. "Chuck Heston had the greatest wave."

Jack winked at Kinski. "You don't have the legs for the role . . . or the chariot."

He turned to MacGregor. "How will the FSE catch up with us?"

"They could use the roadways," Mac said. "But it'll take them quite a ways from the tracks. They'll lose time."

"How else?"

"Well, more than likely, since they let us pass through Glasgow unharmed, they're on our trail already. Supply train, most likely, reconverted commuter train. The older models are pretty slow."

"Let's pray that they have a slow one," Jack said.

"If they pursue us by rail, which is the logical choice," Jack intoned, pointing at the map suspended on the wall, "we'll be ready for them."

"And if they don't?" Kinski asked.

"We're fucked." Jack shrugged. "But that's nothing new."

He turned to Mac. "Get Pheerson and your men into gear. We have to uncouple these suckers within ten minutes. Buddha, Kinski and I will move up the tracks and keep a lookout for any pursuit train."

"What happens if you see one?" Mac asked.

"We stop it," Jack shrugged, leaving the observation car.

"He's nuts," Buddha Chan said.

"He's *good*," Kinski said.

"Nice combination," Buddha said, patting his M-21. "Looks like I'll get a chance to do some sniping."

The train approached the switching yard.

Jack stared out the window of the salon car. The shrubs outside were damp from the mist. A summer moon shone down on the leaves, giving them a gossamer look. His chest still ached from O'Malley's light touch.

He rummaged through a drawer in the car and found an old stogie. He bit off the tip and lit it up.

He inhaled deeply.

Poison invaded his lungs.

It tasted great.

Hell of a world, he thought to himself. But, he added mentally, it was the only one he had.

EIGHTEEN

Crazy Jack, Buddha Chan and Kinski walked slowly down the curling train track, rifles ready, as, behind them in the switching yard, McClennen and Pheerson hustled the men around, uncoupling and recoupling cars as quickly as possible.

"This is madness," Pheerson fumed. "How the hell will I see where I'm going?"

"You could hang your head out the window," McClennen said. "And I'd go a little slower than usual if I were you."

"I won't have much choice, will I?" the thin man spat in the other man's direction. "I'll have enough weight in front of me to change my name to Sisyphus."

MacGregor glowered. "Never mind, man. It's survival we're speaking about here. Do you want to be shot down by some invader?"

"Better that than to wreck a bonnie train," Pheerson said, frowning. "We *are* going to wreck this train, aren't we?"

"It's a possibility, but it'll keep our homeland safe," MacGregor said.

"Safe?" Pheerson growled. "Safe from whom? The FSE boys? The Americans? It's all bollixed up."

MacGregor left the fuming engineer, motioning to McClennen. "Let's see what we can find about."

"Aye." The portly man nodded.

The two men, looking like the figure "ten," walked off to what was once the stationmaster's office.

The old, small shack hadn't been used in years. It was laced with cobwebs and memories.

"Anything?" MacGregor asked.

McClennen padded by an old, kerosene-burning stove. "Just a couple of tins of kerosene."

"Take them."

"Where should I put them?"

"Observation car," MacGregor said flatly.

He walked over to the corner of the eroding shack. No tools. Just a couple of old railroad ties stuck in a corner. They were huge and bulky. MacGregor figured they might come in handy. Lifting the massive metal ties, he tossed them over his left shoulder and marched back toward the train.

On patrol the three Marauders made their way warily alongside the track. Crazy Jack was on one side. Buddha and Kinski were on the other.

"How're things over there?" Crazy Jack hissed.

"Okay, so far," Buddha called.

"Wait a minute," Kinski whispered.

The three men stiffened. From the right of the track they head the roar of an auto engine. A crash. The hissing of a smashed radiator.

Crazy Jack turned his head. He heard a soft, steady sobbing. "This way," he whispered to the other men.

The threesome fanned out in the underbrush.

A few meters to the right of the tracks was a roadway. A pickup truck stood inert, its front wrapped around a telephone pole, squashed in so far as to resemble an old-fashioned concertina.

The driver was slumped over the wheel.

The sobbing was coming from the passenger's seat.

Jack motioned the other two back. Using his recently purloined boots to the best advantage, he trotted, duck-style, to the passenger-side door. Keeping below eyelevel, he yanked the door open.

A small, frail, nine-year-old boy sat there, crying his eyes out.

"Are you going to kill me?" the boy sobbed.

"Not to worry," Jack said.

"I'll die," the boy said. "You can kill me. I don't mind."

Jack's hardened visage collapsed. "It's all right, boy. Nobody will hurt you."

Jack stared at the man behind the wheel. His guts had been blown out. The driver's side of the cab was filled with blood.

"Your daddy?" Jack answered.

"Yes," the boy wheezed.

"A brave man," Jack said.

"He was a shoe salesman," the boy said, puffing his chest out. "He was going to be a manager some day."

"I'm sure he was," Jack said, reaching in and scooping the boy out of the cab of the truck.

"My name is Jack," the orange-haired giant said. "My friends call me Crazy Jack."

"Uh-huh."

"And what's you're name."

"Timmy," the blond-haired boy with a faceful of freckles sniffed. "Timmy McConnel."

Jack placed the boy on the ground. The boy's slender body was wracked with a bad case of the shivers. Jack placed a protective arm around the kid. "You can hug me if you want," Jack whispered.

The boy wrapped himself around Jack's left leg. "Now," Jack whispered, "don't be afraid. I want you to meet two of my very best friends. We're all going to help you. Is that okay with you?"

"I s'pose," the boy whispered.

Jack motioned Buddha Chan and Kinski forward. The two men jogged out of the foliage, their guns drawn.

The small boy's eyes widened in terror. "They have guns!" he cried. "They're going to kill me!"

"No," Jack said. "No, they're here to help you."

"Timmy?" Jack continued, pointing to the short, muscular, round man with sunglasses. "I want you to meet a very good friend of mine. This is Buddha Chan."

The boy looked up at Buddha. "You're not from here, are you?"

Buddha chortled. "Mongolia."

"Where's that?" Timmy asked.

"A land beyond beyond," Buddha said, smiling.

"You look like Aladdin, only shorter," Timmy sniffed.

"We *do* have genies where I come from," Buddha said in a soothing voice.

"I needed a genie," Timmy said, "and there wasn't one around."

"Now there is," Buddha said. "You're safe now."

"It's too late," Timmy wailed.

"It's never too late, son," Kinski said, emerging from the shadows.

"Who are you?" Timmy demanded.

The tall, lanky blond man with the Fabian haircut walked up to the boy. "I am Peter Kinski. I am a soldier. I am your friend."

The trembling Scottish boy stared up into Kinski's weather-beaten face.

"Are you on my side?" Timmy asked.

"You bet. To the maximum."

The boy scrunched his face.

"That means 'yes,' " Kinski added.

The boy relaxed. "Can you help my daddy?"

Kinski glanced inside the truck. The driver, his face the color of chalk, was slumped lifeless over the wheel.

"I don't think so," Kinski said softly. "Daddy's gone to heaven. He'll be happy there, don't you worry. He's probably shaking hands with angels right now."

Timmy rubbed his runny nose. "I hope so. He drove a long time to get me home okay."

Crazy Jack lowered his massive frame onto the ground, kneeling before the boy. "Your daddy was a very brave man," he said. "Who did this to him?"

"A bunch of men I never saw before," Timmy said.

"Tell Crazy Jack about it."

"Well," Timmy began, "my mommy died when I was little. It was during something daddy called Armageddon. Daddy swore a lot. Mommy didn't like it. He always told her that he'd never do it again, by Christ."

Jack stifled a laugh. The boy continued, "Mom got some sort of fever. She died. Dad decided we shouldn't move away. We live here. About a mile away. We have a farm. But things have been going badly. The dirt is rotten. At least that's what my dad says. He says that we have to do what we can and expect the worst. That's why he sells shoes, too. There aren't enough things growing, Dad says. The vegetables and things are rotten and most people don't want to eat them. But everybody needs shoes, Dad says. Once a week we take whatever we can grow and drive up to the big city.''

''What city?'' Buddha asked.

''Helensburgh Upper. It's an old town. Two hundred years old. My daddy says it was the home of Henry Bell.''

''Who's Henry Bell?'' Kinski asked.

''I'm not sure,'' Timmy declared. ''He made a steamboat. *The Comet*, I think. He launched it on January 12, 1812, at Port Glasgow on the south bank of the Clyde. My teacher told me that.''

Jack nodded. ''It sounds like a pretty place.''

''Oh,'' Timmy enthused. ''it *is*.''

The little boy faltered. ''But tonight . . . something bad happened.''

''And what was that?'' Jack asked.

''It was just *weird*,'' Timmy replied. ''We drove into town with our things. We dropped them off as usual. But we went really slow, because there were soldiers all over town. Weird soldiers.''

''Weird in what way?'' Jack asked.

''Well,'' Timmy began, ''they didn't seem as if they *belonged* here.''

''Did they speak funny languages?''

''They did. And they seemed really mean.''

''Then what happened?''

''My daddy decided that we shouldn't stay there. He was nervous, but I don't think he wanted me to know. Daddies are supposed to act strong all the time.''

Jack smiled. ''So what did your daddy do?''

''When the soldiers stopped him, he smiled a lot at them. But he told me to put on my seatbelt and to hold on. No matter what happened I was s'posed to hold on.''

''What did the soldiers do to your daddy?'' Jack asked.

''Well, they asked him a whole bunch of questions.'' Timmy replied.

''About what?''

''About things he didn't know anything about. Planes and trains and people called Freedomers.''

"What did your daddy do when they asked him those questions?"

"He laughed."

"He laughed?"

"That made the soldiers mad."

"I bet it did."

"He said he was a farmer, not a . . . in . . . sur . . . not an insurrrrsomething."

"Insurrectionist?"

"Yeah. He wasn't that."

"What happened then?"

"The soldiers got real mad and told him that we couldn't go home."

"Then what?"

"Then, my daddy got real mad and told them to go to the devil."

"He said that?"

"And a lot more things. He told them to go back where they came from, back in red Russia or somewhere. I know it was a color. It might not have been red."

"And then?"

"Then the soldiers stepped in front of the truck. They were going to hold us for detention, or something like that. They said we were part of the insur . . . well, you know, front that was coming past town tonight. They wanted to ask my daddy a whole bunch of questions."

"And what did Daddy do?"

"He got mad," Timmy said. "Madder than I'd seen him since Mommy died."

"And?"

"And he stepped on the gas and runned over a whole buncha soldiers."

"What did you do?"

"I yelled, 'Look out! Look out! Look out!' 'Cause the soldiers had guns and stuff."

"What happened then?"

"They started shooting at us. I scrunched down in the seat, because glass was flying all over. Bullets came in through my door. I could see them. The door was belching out, you know? Like it was burping?"

"I know," Jack nodded.

"Then I heard my daddy yell."

"He yelled?"

" 'Jesus Christ,' he yelled. And then he yelled some more. He grabbed onto his tummy like he had a stomach ache or something bad. And then I saw the blood."

The boy started to cry.

"I saw the blood coming out of his tummy and I cried. He told me that I shouldn't be crying and that he'd get me home all right and that I should be a man. But I'm not a man yet. I don't think, anyhow. And he kept on driving. He drove real fast. He wanted to get me home. But on the way he started to get sleepy. And whenever his eyes would get to closing, I'd ask real loud, 'Daddy? Do you want to take a nap?' And he'd say, 'No, Timmy.' And then he'd ask me to talk to him, only real loud. So I kept on talking and talking to him. Telling him about what I was doing in school and how I missed Mommy and how I hated the soldiers that shot him and stuff like that."

"And your daddy kept on driving?"

"Until just now."

Jack nodded, looking at the brown-haired young man slumped over the wheel, his intestines hanging out of his stomach, He had been hit by a burst of automatic fire and hit well.

Timmy looked at Jack. "Just now, he fell asleep. He told me to watch out for myself and to be a good boy, and then, all of a sudden, he wasn't driving too well. I yelled at him to watch out for the pole but he hit it anyway."

Jack nodded. He turned to Buddha and Kinski. "We know where they're going to try to hit us now," he said.

"Just dumb luck," Kinski said sadly.

"Maybe." Buddha replied. "Timmy? What are you going to do now?"

"Go home, I guess. With Daddy."

"But Daddy's with the angels," Buddha replied.

"He can't come with me?"

"I don't think so."

Timmy gazed into the truck. "But he's still *here*."

"His body is here, Timmy," Buddha said, walking toward the boy. "But his soul is in Heaven."

"He's dead?" Timmy sniffed.

"He is," Buddha nodded. "But don't worry. He's with your mommy, and someday you'll be with them both. Right now, though, we have to find a place for you to stay."

"What about home?" Timmy said. "Can't I just go home?"

"Do you have any relatives there?" Jack asked. "People who could take care of you?"

"No," Timmy replied after thinking about that for a moment.

The three men stood in silence.

"Tell you what?" Crazy Jack asked. "How would you like to take a train ride?"

"Where?" the boy replied.

"To wherever we go. You'll really like it. We have our own train, and a lot of guns, and we can keep the bad soldiers away."

"I've never been on a train," Timmy confessed.

"Then it's about time you took a grand ride," Jack said enthusiastically.

"And then what?" Timmy asked.

"And then, Timmy," Buddha said, squatting in front of the boy, "you'll go wherever we go. Does that sound like fun?"

Timmy thought hard about the question. "I . . . I guess."

"Good," Buddha said. "come back with us and we'll show you the train."

The three Marauders led the small boy away from the truck and walked with him down the tracks. In the distance the *Royal Scotsman* sat, its engine purring.

"Now isn't that a fine train?" Crazy Jack asked the boy.

"Yes." Timmy nodded. "Are you sure it's okay if I ride on it?"

"I'm positive."

Timmy turned to the road behind him. He raised a small hand and waved it. "Good-bye, Daddy," he whispered.

NINETEEN

"And that's why they call me Shatterhand," MacGregor said, showing the small boy his studded, leather-encased fist as the train picked up speed.

"Pretty neat," Timmy replied.

The soldiers huddled in the salon car as the train highballed it toward Helensburgh Upper. Jack sat with McClennen. "Anything worth picking up at the station?"

"Some kerosene, a few railroad ties."

"Good," Jack nodded. "We'll need them all. How far are we from the town?"

"Another mile or so."

Jack faced Kinski and Buddha. "Take your positions at the windows. I don't want anyone in the rear of the train."

The men nodded and moved the Freedom Fighters into place, the furniture in the car stacked next to the windows.

"What can I do?" Timmy asked.

"You can be a really good boy and sit under that desk," Jack said, pointing to a huge mahogany writing table.

"I can fight," Timmy said defiantly.

"I know you can," Jack said. "But you have to fight when it's proper to. Right now, these men will fight. We want to save you for a bigger battle."

"Okay," Timmy said, sliding under the desk.

MacGregor heaved a sigh. "A feisty one, isn't he?"

"Takes after his father. I'm going up to the engine," Jack said, leaving the car and walking from cubicle to cubicle until he reached Pheerson, a man not at all happy with his station in life.

"This is madness," the gangly man said, his head draped out of the window.

"Don't I know it," Jack said. "Now, if you see *anything* up ahead, tell me."

Jack picked up an M-16 and thrust his head out the left window. "We have to build up speed."

"If we go any faster, we run the risk of derailing the sleeping cars. Now that would be pretty, wouldn't it? Sweet Jeezus in Heaven."

Jack squinted into the darkness. Ahead, a large produce truck backed by several civilian cars was lined across the tracks in the small station area. Flanking the barricade were thirty or more FSE troops.

"Sound the whistle," Jack said.

"You don't think they're going to move that stuff out, do ye?" Pheerson said, stone-faced.

"No," Jack said. "But I want them to know we see what's coming and we'll do what we have to do."

"Crazy Yank," Pheerson muttered, yanking the whistle and pushing the train to full throttle.

The FSE troops at the station watched the train approach, a communal, confident smile on their lips.

Then they heard the whistle.

The FSE men glanced at each other nervously. The train wasn't slowing down. They grabbed their AK-47s and stared at the speeding train. The engine wasn't forward as they had believed. Four long, steel cars were in the lead, barreling toward their barricade.

The leader of the troops, a lieutenant named Dudzek, motioned the men back onto the train station's platform.

Inside the engine Jack yanked Pheerson's head out of the window. "Get down low and brace yourself."

"I can maneuver my own train," Pheerson yelled, shaking off Jack's massive paw.

"Maybe. But can you outmaneuver bullets?"

"Anything they throw at me, I'll take," the feisty engineer said, pushing the throttle down hard.

In the salon car Kinski was the first to spot the barricade. "Hold onto your gonads" he bellowed, "and be ready to return fire."

Under the writing table Timmy stared nervously up at the armed men. "Are we going to hit something?"

MacGregor bent low toward the desk. "It's like a game, Timmy. They try to stop us. We try to go by. Do you understand that?"

"Yessir," Timmy gulped. "But what's a gonad?"

In the engine Jack placed his M-16 in the window. "All right, Pheerson, show me how good you are."

"Better than you'll ever be, Yank," Pheerson yelled.

A screech.

Metal against metal.

Pheerson and Jack bounced around the engine as the sleeping cars smashed through the truck and car barricade. "Oh shit," Pheerson yelled, squatting low. "Hit the deck, boy. Get your face out of the window."

The first car smashed into the barricade.

The truck exploded on impact, its gas tank ruptured by the runaway train. It in turn transformed the cars behind it into thundering fireballs. The air was shattered by the deafening roar of an inferno given full freedom.

"Hot stuff," Pheerson cackled maniacally. He pulled down on the whistle. "Woooooeee," he shrieked, as a wall of flame engulfed the train, plunging ever onward.

The FSE men bellowed in both fear and rage as the train destroyed their barrier. They tried to fire their weapons, but the shards of hot, flaming metal sailing through the air kept their aim askew. The train moved over the remains of the vehicles; cutting, slicing, struggling.

Liquid flame spread over the tracks, licking the train's underbelly.

In the salon car the men held onto their seats. "Open up!" Buddha yelled.

"Rock and roll!" Kinski said, struggling for balance.

The Freedom Fighters in the car unloaded on the FSE troops as the train smashed its way forward.

Glass shattered.

The ka-thunk of metallic debris smashing into the side of the car echoed in their ears.

"Are we going to get through?" MacGregor yelled.

"Who the hell knows?" Buddha answered, squeezing the trigger of his M-21, effectively spraying the station. "This is just going to be one of those nights."

The FSE troops howled in rage.

They choked on the thick black smoke produced by the smashed, squashed barricade.

They ducked the fragments as best they could.

The old train, like some sort of wounded behemoth, refused to stand still. It continued to pound its way through the barricade, sending up showers of sparks and flame.

Before the FSE troops could find a suitable target for their fire, the bullets of the Freedom Fighters sang through the smoke-laden air.

One goon went down, screaming. Then another and another.

The train plunged forward through the ever-expanding inferno. The old station, made of wood, slowly began to sizzle. Tiny tongues of flame began to appear at the base of the building. On the eaves. At the edges of the platform.

The FSE troops, not expecting such a complete rout, were at a loss. They tried to run, but everywhere they turned, they encountered new slices of flame. They tried to fire back, but their eyes made contact with nothing but a rumbling cloud of dense, black smoke. They attempted to save each other, but the air around them seemed to lash out, bringing them bullets and more bullets.

Within seconds the FSE ambush had been destroyed. The train continued on its way, screeching and grinding down the tracks. The FSE troops left behind collapsed in small pools of blood and flame.

This was not warfare, Dudzek thought, as his body toppled into a river of flame. This was brutality.

He fell headfirst into a pool of gasoline. His lungs were choked by white hot fumes. His eyes bubbled up. His skin began to blister. He writhed for a moment or so and then gave way to the sledgehammer effect of the old train.

By the time the reinforcements arrived, there were no comrades there to greet them. Only a shell of a train station that went back two hundred years, the stench of burning flesh, the ashen remains of human skeletons torched beyond recognition and waves of anger and vows for revenge.

In the engine of the sputtering train Jack glanced behind the vehicle. "Well done, Pheerson," he laughed.

"Wasn't bad," Pheerson said, struggling to his feet. "But I'll have you know that we've ruined the sleeper cars."

"How quickly can we get to the next switching station?"

"Five, ten minutes. Why?"

"Pull in and we'll uncouple the sleepers. That little collision we pulled off back there will buy us a little time, but not much."

"So what will we do now?"

"The *Royal Scotsman* will make the supreme sacrifice, Pheerson."

The engineer shot Crazy Jack a fishy look. "Don't worry, Pheerson," Jack said. "This old train just might wind up saving your country."

"You're going to do her in?"

"Afraid so," Jack replied. "But think of it. A train as a national hero."

Pheerson peered up ahead, past the smoldering sleeper cars. "Every train is a hero to me, son."

Jack stuck his head out the engine and surveyed the tracks behind them. Somewhere, he knew, was a train filled with Maximov's goons, out to stop them before they reached the Highlands.

TWENTY

Mamudi and Bee led the speeding caravan over the roadsides of Scotland toward Aberdeen. They were five hundred men strong now, and the number was increasing by five or ten at each town they passed through.

Cutting across the Rampian Mountains on a steep road so as not to encounter the main FSE contingent heading north, Bee began to consider the sheer insanity of the plan.

"We're going to have to thin the ranks," he said, pulling the lead truck over.

"That's just what we need," Mamudi sighed, climbing out of the truck as Bee signaled for the caravan to stop.

Bee addressed the Scots in tow.

"Gentlemen," he began. "I know you're all here because you want to keep the Federated snakes from taking over the oil rigs. And I know you're here at great sacrifice. You're putting your lives on the line. But . . . ''

He paused for a moment. "And here's a big consideration. By this time we've attracted as much attention from FSE intelligence as a parade. Some of you will have to leave the caravan now and secure this road."

The Scots grumbled.

"I know it's not what you planned, but the truth of the matter is, we don't have surprise on our side, only sheer guts and determination. I know that you—of all people—will acknowledge that."

The men in the caravan nodded grudgingly.

"So here's what I propose. One hundred of you remain here at Huntly. We're north of Aberdeen. The FSE troops are coming up from the south. Any troops in pursuit of us will *have* to take this road down to Aberdeen. And when they show up—"

"We'll slaughter them!" one voice yelled.

"Aye," a hundred other voices cheered.

"It won't be as easy as that," Bee said. "You're outmatched and outnumbered. You're going to have to hide yourselves well and come up with any type of booby trap you can devise to slow them down."

"Slow them down?" one old man cackled. "We'll take them out, boy. Most of us here have hunted. What's the difference if you're tracking a fox or a snake?"

"Aye," the men agreed. "We have rope, trees and a lot of road. That, when you add in our guns, should do more than a little to keep the Federated invaders at bay."

"It might help to mine the roads," Bee said. "Do you have explosives?"

"How does dynamite sound?" the old man replied.

"Sounds fine," Bee smiled.

"Then what are you standing around for, hippie? Get down to Aberdeen and kick their fannies out of Scotland for good."

Bee and Mamudi exchanged pleased looks. "All right," Bee replied. "That's just what we intend to do. May the spirits protect you."

"They'll warm us up as well," the old man shouted, producing a flask.

Bee laughed to himself and trotted toward the truck. Mamudi jumped into the passenger's seat, and Bee pulled out, leading most of the caravan with them.

"This is the sloppiest operation I've ever had the misfortune to take part in," Mamudi muttered.

"I know," Bee said. "That's why it might be the most effective."

Mamudi nodded. "You just might be right."

TWENTY-ONE

The train, carrying Crazy Jack, MacGregor, Buddha Chan and Kinski, now bereft of the forward cars, continued on its desperate attempt to reach the Highlands.

"Can't Pheerson get this crate going any faster?" Jack muttered.

"We are heading up steep terrain," MacGregor replied.

"We have company," Kinski said, calling from the observation car located in the back of the train.

The men ran back. Jack saw the dim light of a pursuing locomotive in the mist behind.

"Get all the men forward," he said softly.

The Marauders, little Timmy and the Freedom fighters in the troup ran up to the small dining car located directly behind the engine.

"How will we stop them?" Buddha asked.

"With a little fire, a little risk and a lot of poundage," Jack replied.

The train continued to lurch forward.

"They're gaining on us," Kinski said.

"No problem," Jack said. "McClennen? Where are the canisters of kerosene?"

"Right here, crazy man," the Scot replied.

"Gimme 'em," Jack said.

122

"Don't leave me out of this operation," Kinski insisted.

"I wouldn't want to miss the fireworks either," Buddha smiled, slinging off his weapon and handing it to a startled Timmy. "You watch this well, son," he said.

"Will do, *sir*," Timmy answered, proud of the responsibility.

The three Marauders walked to the back of the train and splashed kerosene over every inch of the observation car. Walking carefully backward, they doused the salon car, the observation car and the formal dining car.

"I think that about does it," Jack said smiling. "Let's get forward."

The three men scrambled forward to the small dining car. "Now," Jack said to McClennen, "I'll need tools to uncouple the cars."

"You can't do that when the train is in motion. That's suicide."

"That's what warfare is about." Jack grimaced.

McClennen reluctantly relinquished the large metal ties they had scavenged.

"If you've never done it before," McClennen said, "it can be a tricky maneuver."

"So come with me" Jack smiled.

"I will."

"You might singe your beard."

"It'll grow back."

The two men walked out of the car. Jack looked over his shoulder. "Buddha? Can you loan me your rifle for a moment?"

The short muscular man in sunglasses walked forward. "No way."

"Then will you do me a favor?" Jack asked.

"That'll be easy." Buddha grinned.

"Open up a burst on the next car," Jack said.

With the train rattling along the bumpy track, the men swaying back and forth, Buddha walked forward. "No problem. It's child's play."

Buddha let spray a burst of bullets from his M-21 into the next car. The car, drenched in kerosene burst into flame. Buddha instinctively backed away. "Jack!" he called, "you're living up to your name."

"And then some," Jack chuckled, watching the flames ignite the ancient furniture and wooden walls. "And this is just the start of it."

Jack watched the flames ignite and dance from car to car. They were towing a three-car inferno. He turned to Buddha. "Tell the men to remain ready for any sappers. Get them to their stations."

"But what about you?"

"I'll do fine." He turned to McClennen. "Give me a tie."

The portly old Scot with the white beard nodded, concerned. "I hope you know what the hell y'er doin', son."

"So do I, McClennen," Jack said, taking the large metal spike, and straddling his own car and the flaming car behind him, he put his massive muscles behind the task of separating the two.

The FSE train behind them was clearly gaining ground.

The tracks beneath the *Royal Scotsman* rumbled ominously.

Jack swayed with every twisting turn.

Jack jammed the tie between the C-shaped couplings linking the cars. The tie stuck. Jack, without benefit of hard machinery or any better tools, yanked the tie back between the swaying, swinging, groaning cars in an attempt to separate the flaming rear cars from the rest of the train.

"Jesus!" he exclaimed as a sudden windshift sent a wall of flame shooting over his head.

McClennen looked on, concerned. "Give it up, lad."

"I can't," Jack grunted, straddling the two cars and hoping for the best. "When was the last time these cars were separated?"

"Two years before the war, at the least," McClennen called.

"Great," Jack whispered, putting his back into it, resembling Hercules trying to clean out the stables of olden times as one of his great tasks.

Behind the train the FSE men continued to gain ground.

"Leave the cars," McClennen called, a startled young Timmy at his back. "They'll burn themselves out."

"Not good enough," Jack replied, his muscles aching. "If the FSE catches us, they'll kill us. Where will your land be then?"

Using the railroad tie as an Olympian crowbar, he continued to work the lock connecting the cars.

He grunted. He sweated. He swore. He pushed some more. Finally he heard a resounding click.

"Got it," he bellowed, still working the connection.

The train jolted.

Crazy jack found himself in a very precarious position indeed.

The cars began to separate between his legs. Within an instant he found himself straddling the two cars, his legs splitting wider and wider, the two cars growing farther and farther apart every precious second.

"Whooah," he yelled, dropping the railroad tie down to the railway beneath his crotch.

"Shit," he bellowed.

"Give me your hand, lad," McClennen bellowed, extending a short, pudgy arm.

"I—I can't reach it," Jack cried, his legs splitting wider and wider. He was a dead man.

"You *have* to."

The cars continued to separate. The disengaged cars, all aflame and beginning to feel the pull of natural gravity, slid slowly away from the chugging engine. The forward cars, guided by the engine, pulled farther up the hill.

"Try!" McClennen called. "Try your damnedest, Yank!!!"

Jack stuck out his hand, still trying to maintain his balance. "I can't, McClennen. Go ahead and kick ass!"

"Jack!" McClennen yelled.

Jack, trying desperately not to lose his balance and plunge onto the tracks whizzing by him below, glanced to his left and to his right. To his right rumbled a moving firestorm held aloft by sturdy, metal wheels. To his left loomed salvation, a fat old man with a frightened young boy standing behind him.

He barely heard Timmy yell to McClennen. "I can do it."

"No, you can't, boy," McClennen replied.

"Let me try!" the boy yelled. "Please let me try. I'm strong. My daddy taught me to be strong."

Jack, both arms outstretched, watched the small boy hoist himself up into McClennen's rotund arms.

"Are you sure, lad?" McClennen called over the din

caused by the moving locomotive slam-dashing down the
track. The boy nodded.

"Grab hold tight, boy," McClennen ordered.

"Get ready, Jack," McClennen called.

Jack grimaced and readied himself. McClennen grabbed
the boy by the ankles and unfurled him over the tracks, the
boy's arms outstretched. Crazy Jack grabbed onto the boy's
tiny hands with one massive paw and felt himself being
yanked off the separating cars. His body flew into the air.

He watched the flaming cars slide back behind him. He
clung for dear life onto the frail youngster, swinging another
large arm around the lad's tiny frame.

"I gotcha," Timmy yelled, triumphant.

McClennen, demonstrating more power than his roly-poly
frame suggested, hurled them both onto the small dining car's
platform with a mighty yank. Both Crazy Jack and Timmy
landed with a huge exhale of breath. They slowly climbed to
their feet.

Crazy Jack stood towering over the boy. "Thank you,
Timmy. Your daddy would be proud."

"You all told me you were saving me for a big fight. A
fight that I'd be ready for."

"That we did," McClennen said, rubbing a ruddy hand
through the boy's flaxen hair.

"Now you get to watch," Crazy Jack said, pointing to the
flaming cars slowly sinking down the tracks.

"What's going to happen?" Timmy asked.

"Those cars are going to hit the bad guys," Jack said.
"The men who sent your daddy to heaven."

Timmy watched awestruck as the wheeled conflagration
slowly made itself small at the rear of the train. There was a
moment of sheer silence.

Suddenly the flame billowed.

"A direct hit." Crazy Jack whispered to Timmy.

"What happened?" Timmy asked.

"Our cars hit their train," Crazy Jack replied.

The flames to the rear of the *Royal Scotsman* grew larger
and larger. They moved forward for a few seconds and then
seemed to peter out. An explosion ripped over the distant
track. And another, and another.

Flames spewed out over the damp countryside. Large,

square, moving slices of hell plunged down off the side of the tracks, rumbling, tumbling down into trees. Tiny, moving fireballs emerged from the train—FSE men screaming their last breaths.

Soon Jack, McClennen and Timmy lost all sight of the fire. The *Royal Scotsman* was picking up steam.

"Will they keep on chasing us?" Timmy asked.

"No," Jack said, "I don't think so."

"What will we do now?" Timmy inquired.

"Well, we'll get our train moving faster and then go onto the Highlands," Jack responded.

"What's up there?" Timmy asked.

"Hopefully," Jack replied, "a whole goddamned army of people just waiting to march."

"Suppose they're not there?"

"Then," Jack said, picking the boy up into his arms, "we'll have to be an army all by ourselves."

TWENTY-TWO

The remnants of the *Royal Scotsman* pulled into the deserted, misty station at Inverness. There was no one there to greet them.

"Doesn't look like we're expected," Kinski said to MacGregor.

MacGregor walked up to the engine. "We'll pull up a bit farther. No true clansman would expose himself to the enemy."

"Whatever you say." Kinski smirked, feeling the mission was already doomed.

The train chugged up a bit farther, stopping in a rural field, barren of structures, populated only by mist and trees. "We'll stand here," MacGregor said.

Kinski, Crazy Jack, Buddha Chan and MacGregor left the train. They stood in the darkness. "There's no one here," Crazy Jack said.

"They're here," MacGregor said.

Within seconds, out of the mist, fifty large-chested men emerged, post-nuclear leaders of the ancient clans of Ross, MacKenzie, MacLeod, and three dozen more.

MacGregor thumped his chest with his good hand and bellowed, "Fellow clansmen, now is the time to come to the aid of true Scotland."

A barrel-shaped man named Sutherland, the spokesman for the group, marched forward. "And how will we do that?"

"Since the war," MacGregor continued, "we've been invaded by Europeans who know nothing of our land. We've been subjugated."

"Like the way we were for years by the English?" Sutherland asked, his red beard almost as long as his backlocks.

"Worse than that," MacGregor stated. "We all know why we're here. I sent word ahead. It's the oil rigs they're after. Rigs we must prevent them from reaching in order to keep Scotland, indeed the whole United Kingdom, out from under their thumb."

"We're not part of the United Kingdom," Sutherland called. "Never were. So why should we fight on their behalf?"

"Because if they fall, you fall—for good," Crazy Jack yelled.

Sutherland, his red hair flaming under a fast-rising sun, faced the intruder, "And who are you?"

"He's an American," MacGregor yelled. "Someone sent to help."

"Tell him to go home," Sutherland called back. "America has never seen fit to help the Scots in the past, so why should she now?"

"Because you are important to the freedom of the entire world," Buddha said.

"And what do we have here?" Sutherland observed. "A Buddha in fighting clothes with sunglasses?"

"He's part of our help," MacGregor responded.

"That makes me feel *so* much better," Sutherland said.

"We don't care whether you give a shit about us or not," Kinski bellowed, stepping into the moonlight. "We've risked our lives for you, flying by the seat of our pants over the polar route to get here. You people can make or break the future. We're here to help you stick it to the FSE."

"What difference does it make to us, Elvis," Sutherland said, "whether it's the FSE or the USA that beats us over the head?"

Kinski shut his mouth, not knowing whether he'd been complimented or insulted.

"A lot," MacGregor intoned. "We want Scotland to be free. The FSE wants you to be subservient."

"The Brits have wanted us to be subservient for centuries." Sutherland laughed. "It's not a new concept."

"*We* can break you out of that concept, that bondage," Jack said dryly. "But it has to be up to you."

"We'll have to think about it," Sutherland said. "We might not be up to fighting for you foreigners. Promises have been broken in the past. Promises will be broken in the future, I'm sure. No matter what country we're cooperating with, we'll be sorely disappointed. Right now, we're happy. We can dig far into our lands and come out all right.

"Maybe, in time, we'll build our homelands back up, and then we can talk about an uprising."

"Time is what we haven't got," Jack said.

MacGregor looked mournfully at those gathered. "Ye don't understand, lads. For the first time in hundreds of years we can establish a *free* Scotland in a *free* U.K., but we have to act quickly."

"We have to discuss it all," said Sutherland. "Although your name be MacGregor, you don't have the slightest light of what it means to be a true Scot. We've been denied our true independence, not only by the Brits but by the voting populace of Scotland. We've been shafted by people we thought should be for us. Why should we feel any different toward you? You ask a lot. We mean to give little. We'll wait for our independence . . . until a true Scot comes along."

The sun disappeared behind the first of a mass of rain-clouds sailing over the Highlands. The land was again bathed in darkness. Mist rose up from the ground to touch the low-hanging clouds.

"And we can't stand here talking all morning," Sutherland added. "A storm is coming up and it looks to be a big one."

"I understand," MacGregor said sadly.

Sutherland softened somewhat. "It's not that we don't trust you, MacGregor. Or your friends. But, right now, we're fine where we are. The Federated sons of bitches keep away from us. They're not familiar with our territory and they don't dare to invade it. For all practical purposes, we don't exist for them. They don't know our numbers or our kind. They don't even know we're here."

MacGregor turned to Jack. "I don't know whether we can pull this off."

"We have to," Jack replied, "or else the whole mission is kibosh."

"Kibosh?"

"Finito. Dead meat. Ended and done. Suicide."

"I understand," MacGregor said.

At that point the blunted dawn was shattered by thunder. "What's that?" little Timmy exclaimed.

"Cobras!" Buddha spat.

"What's that?" Timmy asked.

"Helicopters and a whole lot more!" Jack exclaimed, pushing Timmy to the ground as the whole world around them opened up with explosive fire.

"Get back into the train!" Jack yelled.

"What about the mission?" Buddha demanded.

"We'll get to it, fuck the rest of them." Jack snatched Timmy and ran back to the waiting train.

"Where the hell's MacGregor?" said Crazy Jack.

"We left him behind," McClennen called, "with the rest of the clansmen."

"Shit," Crazy Jack hissed. "But so be it. Let's highball it to Aberdeen. It's up to us to fuck those FSE-ers. With or without the clans."

McClennen nodded. "Aye, sir, but what should I tell Pheerson?"

"Tell him to move like he's never moved before," Jack replied.

"That I will," McClennen said. "But what should I say about the Clansmen?"

"Say that they're *thinking* the matter over," Jack replied.

Jack leaped into the train. He gazed out on the field. It was deserted. The clansmen had disappeared as if they had never materialized in the first place.

The two Cobra gunships rose up from behind the trees, like angry wasps, their machineguns tearing up the turf alongside the train.

"Tell Pheerson to get going!" Jack bellowed.

"He's dead!" McClennen yelled from the forward part of the train. "Shot full of holes!"

"Can you operate this thing?" Jack cried.

"That I can, but what about those *machines* above us?"

"Buddha? Kinski?" Jack said, turning to the two Marauders.

Buddha scratched his fuzzy head calmly. "Say no more. Mr. Kinski? Care to engage in some target practice?"

"You got it, Buddha," Kinski grinned.

A soft rain was falling.

"I don't even know where they got those things," Jack hissed.

"Hey, there were U.S. bases all over Europe," Buddha said. "At least they stole the best."

"Are you always this optimistic?" Jack grunted.

"Sure. It helps while away the hours."

As McClennen ran up to the engine, Buddha and Kinski leaped out of the train. Kinski grabbed his trusty AK-47 and Buddha grabbed an M-60. The two men hunched up next to the train. A soft rain began to fall, soaking them to the skin.

"Doesn't the sun ever shine in this country?" Kinski hissed.

"It doesn't seem that way."

"This is going to ruin my hair," Kinski said, feeling the moisture force his pompadour lower and lower onto his forehead. "I'm pissed now. Really pissed."

The Cobras zoomed over the stationary train, their machineguns spitting out streams of lead down onto the damp ground.

"Weather's working for us," Buddha said, slowly lifting his assault rifle. "No sun. No sky. No light."

"Think they're using night scopes?"

"Don't think so. Not by the way they're firing. I think this was a last-minute deal. They expected to nail us on the tracks back there."

"You know the drill?" Kinski asked.

"Don't I ever," Buddha said, grinning. He raised the machinegun and started humming a ditty along the lines of "You take the high road and I'll take the low road," substituting the words "You take the tail end and I'll take the rotors."

The ground around them coughed up mud and hunks of grass. The train windows were shattered, pulverized by round after round of fire.

"Ready?" Buddha asked, rolling onto his back.

"Ready," Kinski said, using the train as back support for his crouching position.

"Let's do it," Buddha muttered, squeezing the trigger on the M-60. His body squirmed in the rapidly forming sea of mud as one of the two Cobras swooped in for another pass.

Kinski, grinning, propped himself up and began to rock and roll.

The Cobra was taken by surprise.

Its gunners abruptly stopped firing.

The massive chopper tried to veer away from the train at the last minute.

"FNGs behind the guns," Buddha yelled. "Let's fucking nail their hides."

Both men continued to fire, gritting their teeth as the noise from the guns and the chopper shook the tranquil air around them.

The men couldn't see their hits, but they felt them. They could picture the tiny slugs smashing into the whirling, spinning blades of the over-confident gunship.

A cough.

A sputter.

A small puff of smoke from the rotor blades.

In the confusion caused by the firefight and the rainstorm, they heard someone yell. It wasn't in English. It was in panic.

They heard the Cobra's engine stutter. The flying machine veered suddenly to the right. It began to tilt this way and that, trying in vain to stabilize itself. The two men on the ground continued to send round after round slamming into the bellowing metal beast.

The copter began to lose altitude as well as direction, struggling ineptly to right itself, to keep itself from spinning like the teacup ride at Disneyland.

Buddha saw one body tumble from the Cobra. It hit the ground with a resounding thud a hundred meters away.

"That's all she wrote," Kinski said, removing his finger from the trigger and slamming another magazine into the AK-47.

Buddha eased up as well, feeling mixed emotions, watching an army chopper, the kind of chopper he had depended on for air support for so long, lose all control.

The Cobra slammed down into a bevy of trees with a teeth-grinding screech.

Metal crumbled.

Trees groaned, splintered and gave way. The out-of-control copter blades sliced through the foliage, sheering off the Cobra frame and going into low orbit as they pounded into the earth.

A silence.

Then a mushroom cloud of fire, fuel and charred remains erupted from the darkness, illuminating the entire forestland in a hellish, red glow.

Buddha Chan flipped down his shades and scanned the skies for the other Cobra. It was nowhere to be seen. "Let's get back on board and get the hell out of here," Chan yelled, tumbling up out of the mud.

"Yeah, right." Kinski nodded. "We're easy marks in this light."

Jack stood nervously in the dining car. "Done?"

"One down. One pulled a disappearing act," Buddha said. "I don't like that."

The startled Freedom Fighters in the car gaped at the two men. "Stay on watch," Kinski told them. "We may have a very big mosquito on our tail."

The train lurched to life and slowly pulled away from the Highland locale.

Jack moved over to Timmy, who was sitting awestruck near a shattered window, watching the still-erupting wreckage behind the train.

"Scary, huh?" Jack said.

"And how," Timmy replied. "Crazy Jack? Why didn't those men come with us? The clansmen?"

"I don't know, son. They had their reasons, I suppose."

Timmy nodded. "Should I get back down under the desk for a while?"

"I think that would be a good idea," Jack said nodding.

The small boy scrambled from his seat and skittered under the desk.

Jack stood and walked over to Kinski and Buddha. "What a mess," Buddha said.

"It's going to get messier," Jack said.

"You think MacGregor is all right?" Kinski asked.

"Hope so," Jack replied. "Jesus, this whole mission sucks. Total fugazi. We could have just stayed home and slammed our dicks with a fucking mallet for all the good we're doing."

"You know what intrigues me?" Buddha said.

"I give up," Jack groused.

"The FSE troops have a working air force. U.S. equipment."

"I *did* notice the Cobras," Jack said, sarcastically.

Buddha chuckled. "Don't get pissed off at me, Jack. But here's the deal. If they have Cobras in working order—very *good* working order—Cobras we knew nothing about, what other goodies might they have flying?"

"We'll know soon enough," Jack sighed.

"The second Cobra," Kinski said grimly.

"You can bet it just didn't disappear for the hell of it," Jack said.

"We're nailed," Buddha said.

"Aww, fuggit," Jack said, "we've been nailed before."

TWENTY-THREE

Bee and Mamudi led the small caravan to the docks at the wind-swept town of Aberdeen. Once a prosperous town, a ship-building town, Aberdeen had taken a hard economic blow during the early 1970s when there was no need for new vessels. Only the discovery of oil kept the town prosperous, with most of its men signing up to work on the big rigs.

The hundred cars and trucks pulled into the center of the shipyard. There was no sign of the other Marauders. No sign of MacGregor and his clansmen. No sign of the FSE. Nothing greeted them but torrential rain, fog and large, choppy waves smashing into the pier.

"I don't like this," Mamudi said.

"You can't always have what you want," Bee said, swinging out of the truck.

The assembled Scots emerged from their vehicles, holding their weaponry; everything ranging from old, rickety M-1s to IRA-smuggled M-79s.

"What are your orders, Captain?" a wiry young man asked.

Bee smiled. Rank didn't matter at this point. "Get the men positioned in those buildings," he said, pointing to the two groups of shanties flanking the entranceway to the shipyard. "If any FSE troops show up, hold your fire until I say so. We'll let them walk up to the yard unscathed for as long as possible. Then we let them know what the Scots are all about, eh?''

"That we will. Captain," the wiry lad said, running off to spread the word among the men.

"We're in deep shit here," Mamudi said.

"Freddie," Bee said, "you're a religious man, aren't you?"

"I try to be."

"If my Creator, my spirits, or your Allah, put us into this situation, he must have a reason for it. We will overcome the hordes. We have our gods behind us, you and I."

Mamudi smiled. "I think the occasion calls for a new eye."

He reached into his soaked shirt pocket and produced the insignia of the Navy SEAL. "I think it's about time I lived up to my reputation," he said, smiling.

"Let's get the explosives," Bee said.

Braving the swirling, slicing shards of rain, the two men ran to a truck carrying one hundred pounds of dynamite. Each stick was plastic encased.

"We have to wire these boys together," Bee said.

"Trust me," Mamudi said. "I've been dealing in explosives all my life."

They turned toward the dock and spotted a small skimmer, a pleasure boat once used by tourists who loved the area. Sleek. Easy to maneuver. Fast.

"Do you think we can get that thing operating?" Bee asked.

Mamudi smiled. "If it's fueled and seaworthy," Mamudi replied, the raindrops slowly trickling down the large crease in his forehead. "It won't take me long to get it running."

"Good," Bee said. "if no reinforcements show up in the next thirty minutes, we take that boat out, loaded with dynamite and do in the first platform. According to the map, it's about five miles out. How fast can we reach it?"

"Judging from the weather conditions and the weight of the explosives, I'd say seven minutes. But to go out there alone would be suicide, Bee."

"Not necessarily."

"What kind of fuse do you want me to set with the explosives?"

"Rig up a timer for eight minutes."

"That's cutting it close."

"We've been cutting it close since we got here."

"It'll be a floating time bomb."

"I know that. Let's get the explosives aboard."

At the Aberdeen station the remnants of the *Royal Scotsman* pulled in unscathed.

Crazy Jack, Buddha Chan, Kinski and the rest waited a long minute before they disembarked.

"This is very confusing," Buddha said. "The FSE greeting party hasn't arrived."

"They could be here and aren't showing themselves," Kinski said, leaping onto the station, training his AK-47 this way and that.

"They're here." Crazy Jack intoned, leading Timmy from the train. "You can be sure of it. Let's head for the shipyard. Timmy? You take my hand and stay with me."

"What if something happens?" the small boy asked.

"Then we'll fight together, all right?"

The boy shook his head up and down. "It's *all right* with me, Crazy Jack."

The small band of Freedom Fighters, a bloodied McClennen in their ranks, marched cautiously toward the long-abandoned shipyard. The rain churned around them, slamming into their clothing, dripping down into their socks and shoes. Above them a gray, angry sky tossed and turned.

The small group padded toward the shipyards. They spotted the caravan.

"They made it," Buddha exclaimed.

"Thank God for small favors," Crazy Jack declared.

The men ran forward, Crazy Jack in the lead, as Mamudi and Bee finished loading the explosives onto the boat. Mamudi was already inside, hotwiring the engine. "It'll be fine," he said, checking the gauges.

"And we'll be fine," Bee said, glancing up at his fellow Marauders. "Backup's arrived."

Bee walked forward toward the men, his own troops still carefully hidden. "I thought you fellows would never get here." He smiled.

"We all shared that feeling," Buddha said.

"Timmy," Crazy Jack said, "I'd like you to meet Tom Bee. He's an American Indian."

"Really?"

"Really," Tom Bee replied, looking down at the boy.

"Timmy is quite a soldier," Crazy Jack said. "He saved my life."

"You did, did you?" Tom asked.

"Sorta. Do you fight cowboys?" Timmy asked.

"I fight your enemies now," Bee said.

"Great," the little boy exclaimed, spying Bee's crossbow. "A bow and arrow?"

"Of a kind," Bee replied, glancing at Jack. "MacGregor?"

"Gone."

"The clansmen?"

"Let's just say they're MIA."

Bee looked around the dock. "So it seems that we're in a no-win situation here."

Jack nodded. "Looks that way. Where are your men?"

"In the sheds, flanking the entranceway."

"Good move."

Bee glanced toward the boat. "I figure if we take out the first platform, it'll be a statement."

"It'll also be a pain in the ass for the FSE," Kinski added. "The next platform is fifty miles north."

Bee nodded. "It doesn't look like we're going to do any real harm to them, does it?"

"Symbolically," Buddha announced. "It'll shake them up a bit."

"But not enough," Bee said. "Well, it's been nice knowing you."

"Where the hell do you think you're going?" Crazy Jack demanded.

"Out to sea," Bee said over his shoulder, walking toward the boat. "Okay, Freddie, outta there."

"What?"

Bee reached down two mighty arms and yanked the startled Mamudi out of the boat. "I said *out*," Bee intoned.

"Hey, I'm the Navy man," Mamudi yelped.

"I have two good eyes, Cyclops," Bee growled.

"You bastard."

"No," Bee said, revving the boat's engines. "I can trace my family tree back three hundred years. You take care of yourself, Freddie. You're a good man. You'll have to whip those boys into shape . . . physically and *spiritually*."

Mamudi watched Bee pull out of the harbor. "You sono-fabitch. You planned this! Get back here! I rigged that boat! It's *mine*."

Bee shook his head slowly. "Was yours."

The small boat filled with explosives, Bee at the helm, smashed into the angry North Sea.

"Where's the Indian chief going?" Timmy asked.

"Bee!" Mamudi shouted. "This is really fucked! You can't do this! You'll never get back! You'll never get back alive!"

"I will," Bee yelled into the wind. "It's up to you to keep me alive."

Crazy Jack, Buddha and Kinski ran up to Mamudi.

"He's going to kill himself," Mamudi muttered.

"He knows what he's doing," Crazy Jack said. "He's a soldier. Older and more experienced than all of us. He knew what he was doing when he signed on."

Mamudi bit his lip. "But it's . . . it's not fair."

"Bullshit's never fair," Kinski said. He yelled into the howling wind. "Go get 'em, chief."

Timmy ran up to the men. "Get 'em, chief! Get 'em!" He began waving his hands frantically.

The Marauders waved their hands high in the air. "Yeee-haaw," they screamed.

Bee waved back, smiling. The boat slowly disappeared into the angry sea.

"I hope he makes it," Mamudi said.

"What do you mean?" Crazy Jack asked.

"He has an eight-minute time operating." Mamudi sighed. "In the best of conditions he'd have a sixty-second playtime. In that ocean? Jack, he's not used to the ocean. He's from the West."

"I have a feeling he's used to anything," Jack replied.

"Christ!" Kinski spat. "He's not used to that!"

A Cobra gunship reared up from behind Aberdeen, its engines growling, its gunners ready.

"Down! Everybody down!" Buddha bellowed.

Crazy Jack pulled Timmy down to the wooden pilings, shielding the tiny boy with his body. The rest of the Marauders and the Scottish Freedom Fighters hit the dirt as well.

The Cobra chose not to strafe the area. Instead, it sailed out over the angry North Sea in pursuit of Tom Bee.

TWENTY-FOUR

The Marauders watched the Cobra slice out over the angry North Sea. They heard a ka-thump behind them.

The center of the Aberdeen shipyard blew away.

"FSE troops!" Mamudi shouted.

The men ran for cover, Crazy Jack pulling Timmy behind him. Ka-thump. Ka-thump. Ka-thump.

The men looked up. Surrounding the shipyard were a dozen APCs filled with FSE troops. In addition, a half dozen six-by's lined the area.

"Looks like we're dead meat," Crazy Jack said.

"Indeed you are," came a voice from the mist. "On your feet. All of you."

The men looked around. A thin, pasty-faced man holding an Uzi stepped forward. "And please don't try for your weapons. It would be useless. I have you surrounded and outnumbered."

The Marauders and Timmy slowly got to their feet.

"And who, may I ask, are you?" Jack said.

"Montrose," the pasty-faced man replied. "Your main source of information."

"As well as the main source of information to the FSE," Jack muttered.

"I try to play both sides to my advantage," the thin, acne-scarred man replied.

The FSE men lining the shipyards scrambled from their vehicles and began to advance.

"And what's your real name? Jack asked.

"In these parts of the country," Montrose replied, "I am known as King Edward."

"Jesus Christ," Crazy Jack exclaimed, "*you're* the toady king?"

"That I am," the man replied, making sure his weapon was trained upon them all. "I can't take the chance to wind up like my predecessors. I decided, early on in the game, to take out every insurance policy available. Your bodies will insure my reign for years and years to come. I'm stupid sometimes. Scared a lot of times. But I value my life. Nobody is stupid enough to want a premature ending to a great story."

"Whoopie," Kinski muttered.

"You don't have to have hard feelings about it all, Yank," King Edward intoned. "It's something you have to learn to expect, isn't it? I mean, this is warfare, right?"

"In the basest sense of the word," Buddha replied.

"Now here's what I have planned," King Edward said flatly. "O'Malley and his kind don't suspect me of having such Machiavellian ways. I still have to prove myself to them. They'll be surprised by this sudden show of strength, I grant you. But on the whole, I think they'll be well pleased. My troops will destroy you here. My copter will take out your man before he reaches the rig. I'll come home a hero. I'll be a *king* in the grandest sense of the word. It'll also send a message to the Freedom Fighters in the U.K. as well as their supporters in the States. Beware. Beware the once and future King of England. He'll have no tolerance for subversive types. He's a member of the FSE and proud of it."

"Great," Crazy Jack muttered.

"And now," King Edward said, training his Uzi on the men, "prepare to become martyrs for the cause."

He raised his weapon.

The wind seemed to scream out, shrieking a mournful noise.

All the Marauders seemed to cock their heads.

King Edward did as well.

"Witches!" Timmy whispered. "Witches are coming."

"Not witches, boy," Crazy Jack whispered, "something *else*."

That wasn't wind howling. That was a banshee screeching. A gathering call for revenge.

"What the hell is that?" Kinski muttered, shivering from the cold.

"I don't know," Buddha replied.

"It's the devil himself," Crazy Jack exclaimed.

Timmy smiled, now understanding the sound. "Naaah. It's just bagpipes."

"Bagpipes!" King Edward exploded.

"Aye," came a voice from behind him.

A shot rang out. King Edward's skull exploded. The men and the boy ducked to get out of the way as several ounces of semisolid matter flew out toward them.

"Yucch," the small boy exclaimed.

King Edward's sallow body twitched and twirled through the rain-streaked air as he tumbled and turned, falling to the ground.

"That's one for the good guys," Jack whispered.

King Edward's body collapsed in a bloody heap at the Marauders' feet.

Out of the stormy, swirling mist stepped a familiar figure. MacGregor, a .45 in his hand.

"Mr. MacGregor!" Timmy cried. "I thought you'd been smushed!"

"Not by a longshot, laddie. Listen."

The sound of the bagpipes grew louder. Louder. Bansheelike piping, guaranteed to make a grown man cower.

"Look, over the hill," MacGregor said proudly. "It's the gathering of the clans."

From beyond the docksides of Aberdeen arose two thousand strong men, piping, chanting, carrying weapons ranging from M-16s to Thompsons.

"You talked them into it!" Jack exploded.

"They didn't need too much talking to," MacGregor said.

The FSE troops, rounding the ship yard, were taken by surprise.

Mamudi ran into the open area. *"Now!"* he cried. "The captain says to get them *now!*"

The Scots hidden in the shanties emerged and fired into the FSE men as the Highland Scots marched proudly into the fray. The FSE troops, outflanked on all sides, didn't exactly know where to turn, their leader missing in action. Their APCs' .50 caliber machinegun turrets spun frantically around. The Highlanders lit sticks of dynamite and began tossing them like firecrackers. The APCs found themselves besieged on all sides.

One, two, three of them exploded in the confusion. The men in the APCs tumbled out of the vehicles, guns drawn.

Both the Highlanders advancing and the Freedom Fighters at the dock charged, yelling in Gaelic.

Mamudi, Buddha, Crazy Jack and Kinski exchanged knowing looks. "Let's get into it." Mamudi grinned, unsheathing his knives. "It's hand-to-hand time."

The Marauders trotted into the fray, guns drawn, knives ready.

MacGregor stayed behind with the boy. "Will they win?" Timmy asked.

"No question about it," MacGregor said, putting his mighty good hand around the boy.

"Now you wait here for me, okay?" he said, raising his .45.

"Okay."

MacGregor trotted off into the mist.

The Marauders charged into the battle.

Within minutes there was no one left alive on the docks of Aberdeen but Scots and four lone Americans. The Highlanders marched down to the docks and embraced the remaining Lowland troops.

"We were beginning to think you'd never arrive," McClennen said, walking up to Sutherland.

"We had trouble negotiating the roads," Sutherland smiled, embracing the small, rotund man.

All the men walked toward the edge of the dock, wondering about Tom Bee, hoping for the best, fearing the worst. Out from beyond the raging waters of the North Sea, they could hear gunfire.

It didn't look good.

TWENTY-FIVE

Under the cover provided by the dense fog, the high seas and the thick rain, Tom Bee guided his small boat toward the first of the oil platforms towering in the swirling North Sea.

The Cobra, buffeted by the high winds, pursued him, straffing the water around him regularly. The growling gunship boasted two rocket pods on each side, each capable of sending out 2.5-inch rockets. The XM-21 systems, miniguns, sprayed out two thousand rounds per minute. Solid electronics. Bee grimaced as round after round sliced into the sea. The only thing he had going for him was the weather and the FSE pilot, a novice to the area.

He could only count on the spirits to guide him to the spot where he would be the most help to the world. He knew the spirits would oblige. He had nothing more of his life to give.

After a few minutes. He spied it—an Olympian, skeletal form arising from the sea. The platform.

The waves slashed against the bow of the boat as he cranked it forward. The bullets lashed around him as the Cobra, hampered by the fog and the storm, continued its relentless pursuit.

Bee gritted his teeth, knowing now that there was only one tactic left to him. He lashed the boat's wheel on a steady course, using a bunji cord. The rudder was locked in now; the boat aimed straight at the base of the rig.

Bee turned from the helm and settled down into the boat, drawing his mini-crossbow. He smiled grimly as the Cobra dove down through the fog again, strafing mindlessly the white-capped waves around him.

Bee reached into the plastic-encased mound of explosives and produced a dry stick of dynamite. Using his body as cover, he lashed it hastily to one of his arrows and lit the fuse. Jamming the arrow into his mini-crossbow, he flung himself around on the deck and took careful aim at the Cobra. He prayed that the spirit of the eagle would guide his eye. Allow the arrow to fly free.

The Cobra, as if on cue, spotted Bee and lunged for him, swooping low over the water.

Bee squinted his eyes, seeing the machineguns flare up from the mighty airborne warship. He felt the bullets slice into his legs. He yanked the trigger of the crossbow. As he did so, he felt the bullets penetrate his abdomen. He tumbled onto the deck, bullets taking out shards of wood and plastic all around him.

He grinned to himself. The spirit of the eagle appeared to him, allowing him to die knowing that his aim was true. He kept his eyes and ears open long enough to hear the Cobra explode with a metallic shriek. Bits of flaming debris began to fall all around him.

The boat continued onward. He was on a time fuse, he knew. The mission would be successful.

He slowly, painfully pulled his blood-spattered body upward in time to see the boat enter the underbelly of the rig. At that point, a fierce, white heat invaded his body. His ears went deaf at the first hint of a bang.

He didn't hear the explosion. He only half-witnessed it. He felt the skin on the back of his body spiral up as the explosive charge in the boat detonated. His consciousness tumbled forward over the bow as the explosion took his body upward, tumblesaulting him into space, into the North Sea.

Bee managed to stay afloat long enough to see the traveling bomb careen into the rig, setting it off.

The gas lines caught first. Tongues of flame shot up from

the underbelly of the skeletal beast. The top section went into low orbit with a resounding ka-boom.

Dense black smoke mingled with the low clouds. Explosion after explosion rocked the North Sea as the oil rig unleashed all its pent-up, unspent energy. Before long, the sea around it was hot and churning.

What was left of Tom Bee's existence bobbed and weaved in the bubbling sea for a brief second. Then it disappeared. And, soon after, so did the oil platform.

Back at Aberdeen, the Marauders and the remainder of the Freedom Fighters stared into the deep fog. A sudden starburst shook the foundation of the sea. Bright, orange light sliced through the gloom like a red hot knife. They heard the resounding blast a moment after spotting the volcanic eruption.

"He did it," Crazy Jack gasped.

"He's not coming back," Mamudi muttered.

It was so.

The men turned as one and walked away from the North Sea.

Victorious.

In pain.

TWENTY-SIX

The Marauders, followed by MacGregor and his Freedom Fighters made the long trek down to London in a week's time, driving out any last remnants of FSE support on the way and rounding up hundreds of other able-bodied men who wanted to join the cause.

By the time they reached the city limits, all traces of the FSE command were gone. Ian O'Malley was nowhere to be found. The city suddenly found itself freed from the bonds of subjugation. —

Crowds had gathered in the streets to greet the burgeoning caravan as it paraded into the city, cheering the Marauders as well as the suprised, elated clansmen.

The Maruaders marched in file silently. They acknowledged the cheering crowds, but their hearts were nowhere to be found. Their hearts remained five miles off the coast of Aberdeen, contained in the remains of Tom Bee.

Timmy clutched Crazy Jack's hand, staring at the throngs. "Crazy Jack?"

"Yes, son?"

"You don't seem very happy."

Jack forced a smile. "I am, Timmy. We won."

"But the Indian chief? He's not here with us, is he?"

All the Marauders reacted to the small child's statement as if they had been slapped. They continued to march onward. "He *is* here," Freddie Mamudi said, leaning down toward the boy.

"How come I can't see him then?" the boy asked.

Mamudi smiled. "Because we have him hidden . . . in here," Mamudi said, loud enough for all his colleagues to hear. He pointed to his heart.

"Tom Bee was a very special person, Timmy. He was a man who was only partly in this world."

"I don't get it," the boy said.

"He was here with us," Mamudi explained. "But part of him was always up there. In the spirit world. He was a man who could talk to the wind. Listen to the trees. Understand the rain. He's gone to that world now, but he was with us long enough to leave a little bit of him behind. Part of his soul is in all of us now. As long as we live on this earth, as long as we take a single breath of air, Tom Bee lives."

Buddha suddenly smiled. "I like that thought."

Kinski found himself laughing. "I *feel* that thought."

Crazy Jack nodded. "I think Tom knew that this would be his last mission. All he wanted us to do was pull together, get into shape as a team. He was the oldest. He had seen a lot more crap than we ever had. He was our guide this time out."

"He'll be our guide for a long time to come," Mamudi replied.

"So now the Indian chief is with my mommy and daddy," Timmy said.

"I bet he is," Crazy Jack said.

Timmy squeezed Jack's callused hand. "I like that. He'll protect them. They'll never be hurt by bad people anymore."

"He'll protect us all," Crazy Jack said.

The Marauders found themselves smiling at the memory of the sometimes sullen, always watchful and protective Tom Bee. They began to wave back at the cheering throngs. They found the cheers as intoxicating as fine wine.

The procession found its way to Buckingham Palace. The crowds cheered and called for Shatterhand. MacGregor slowly ascended the stairs in front of the palace. The crowd fell silent. The bearded, burly Scot took a deep breath. He needed no microphone. His voice seemed to plug into the air and resonate like thunder from Olympus. Above him, rainclouds swirled ominously. A sultry summer's wind wafted through the palace grounds.

"My countrymen," he boomed. "We have driven out the invaders."

The crowd cheered. MacGregor waved them into silence. "We are now truly a United Kingdom. We have beaten the Federated States of Europe. We will no longer be enslaved by their desires. But now, more than ever, we must pull together to insure our future freedom.

"We must work at rebuilding our country. Rebuilding our armed forces. Reorganize the police. The FSE will retaliate, make no mistake of that. We must flex our muscles and be ready for the next assault."

The crowd yelled as one.

"And," MacGregor said, "be forewarned, there will be many hardships to endure, but they will be *our* hardships. *Ours.* We stand or fall on our own initiative. Every man, woman and child in this great land of ours must raise a clenched fist and vow, 'Never again!' "

"Never again!" the crowd roared.

"We drove out the enemy this time, but only through the intervention of our allies, the United States."

He pointed his shattered hand at the Marauders. "These brave men, some of the finest soldiers in America, came to our aid to organize and mobilize. They risked their lives for us all. They fought in situations many sane man would turn from. These are our allies, my countrymen. These will forever be our allies."

A wave of cheers arose as the Marauders turned and faced the crowd.

"And *they*—as well as *we*—suffered a terrible price for our victory. We lost many a man. Brave ones all. They lost a *brother*. They are now four. They began as five. Five fingers in one clenched fist, setting out to smash the hold of the FSE. We mourn our fallen comrades. We must also mourn for a man called Thomas Bee. A man who traveled thousands of miles to help a people he knew not. To fight in a land he knew not. To sacrifice himself for a cause that was bigger than any nationality, stronger than any country, greater and grander than any ruler, no matter how rich or how adorned . . . *freedom.*"

The crowd roared, tears falling openly. At that point a warm wind sliced through the palace grounds. The clouds above parted for one brief moment, and rays of sunlight fell onto the throng. The people of London drifted off into silence, staring at the sun. A rainbow slowly cut across the sky, slithering toward the earth, landing at a point unseen.

The Marauders felt the sun on their faces and stared upward. "How do you like that, Tom?" Mamudi whispered.

Timmy clutched Jack's hand. "The Indian chief! I saw the Indian chief riding on the rainbow!"

Jack wiped a single tear from his face. "I bet you did, son. Wave to him from all of us."

As the little boy began waving frantically at the rapidly disappearing rainbow, MacGregor continued, "We must be proud of our achievements in the past two weeks, but we also must be cautious. There will be treachery afoot, have no two minds about that. The FSE will try to insinuate themselves into our ranks, try to undermine our every move, and it is for *this* reason that I propose that these brave Americans, the Marauders, be allowed to use London as their base of operations, to help *all* of Europe accomplish what we have done!"

The crowd began to chant, "Marauders! Marauders!"

The four remaining team members smiled and waved at the crowd.

"And now," MacGregor said, "we must go about the task of reorganizing our government. Our own king, Edward, was in the employ of the FSE."

The crowd began to hiss.

"In fact, Edward tried at every turn to annihilate us, to destroy the mission, to keep us from achieving our goal. He died in battle, at Aberdeen. It was *I* who shot him. I am not proud of that fact. A king is a king. But I am not sorry about that fact, either."

A hush fell over the crowd.

MacGregor swallowed hard. "And now it is up to you, the people, to guide this country forward. What is your response?"

"The king is dead!" came a voice.

"Long live the king!" the crowd thundered.

MacGregor was taken aback. "I don't understand," he said to Crazy Jack.

"I think you've finally gotten yourself a Scottish king," Jack grinned.

"What?"

"Long live King Shatterhand!" Crazy Jack yelled.

"Long live King Shatterhand!" the crowd cried. "Shatterhand! Shatterhand!"

"Jesus, Mary and Joseph," MacGregor muttered.

"I hope you'll ask us to your coronation," Jack laughed.

Mamudi, Buddha and Kinski began to chuckle.

"And here we thought you were just a big, pig-headed kinda guy," Kinski said.

"You never told us," Buddha said. "I could have bowed a lot more on the train."

"I would have worn a classier eyeball," Mamudi added, "and maybe have decorated my scar."

"Quit it," MacGregor growled.

"Long live the king!" the crowd cheered.

MacGregor turned and faced the crowd. He tried to speak but the words stuck in his throat. The crowd surged forward. The clansmen, clad in tartans, allowed them to pass. MacGregor found himself faced with thousands of well-wishers, eager to follow his leadership.

The air was suddenly filed with the sound of bagpipes.

The kingdom was truly united.

Jack turned to Mamudi. "You hungry?"

"I was just thinking the same thing."

Buddha shrugged. "Think there are any good dives nearby?"

"Depends if you like fish and chips" Kinski said.

"*I* do," Timmy replied.

"Then," Jack said, lifting the boy up onto his massive shoulders, "would you care to join us?"

"You bet."

The four Marauders and the tiny boy waded their way through the crowd.

"Looks like everything is going to be fine," Jack smiled.

"Yeah," Buddha said, adjusting his sunglasses, "for a week or two."

"Let's make the most of it," Mamudi said.

"What kind of fish do they use in fish and chips, anyhow?" Kinski asked to no one in particular.

Behind them the new king was greeted by his subjects.

A chapter of history had closed.

TWENTY-SEVEN

Maximov sat in his palace, drumming his neatly trimmed nails on the armrest of a Chippendale chair, sacked from one of England's finest country houses. A toady named Bjorn stood next to the radio, ready to turn off the station as soon as the bearlike Maximov blinked. The newly inaugurated Radio Free Europe, now based in the U.K., was broadcasting all too loudly and all too clearly.

A new king was being crowned in England.

Good King Shatterhand.

A man with a booming voice and a hand withered through torture. A man who vowed to fight the Federated States to his last, dying breath. A man who pledged his allegiance to the newly formed Freedom Fighters' Pact with Free America. A man who allowed an American Special Forces team to use his own country as its homebase.

The coronation seemed to go on forever. The cheers of the people were volcanic. Maximov waved to his toady. The toady switched off the radio, allowing Maximov to simmer in silence for a moment.

"Contact O'Malley. I want him here," Maximov whispered. " I want all of my Western European operatives here. Immediately."

"Yes, Chairman Maximov," the toady said, saluting. "And should I add anything else to the message?"

"Tell them . . . ," Maximov began, "tell them we will plan a strategy. A new strategy. A strategy that will destroy the King of England and one that will leave each of the four American Marauders drowning in his own blood."

"Yes, Chairman Maximov."

"One more thing," Maximov added. "Tell them we will no longer present ourselves as a benign dictatorship. Anyone who opposes us dies. Anyone who can bring the head of even one Marauder into our possession will be treated like a prince."

"Yes, Chairman Maximov."

Maximov watched the man skitter out of the room. He leaned back into his chair. He wondered what he would be served for dinner. He hoped it wouldn't be liver. God, how he hated liver.

A small kitten pranced into the room, one of the palace's new litter. The kitten snuggled up to Maximov. He smiled, glancing down at the small wad of fur. He reached down and began stroking it.

Maximov chuckled.

Then he broke its neck.

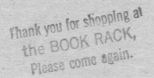